THE OUTCASTS

Also by March Hastings

Abnormal Wife
Again and Again
The Boys of Brigham Dee
By Flesh Alone
Crack-Up
The Demands of the Flesh
Design for Debauchery
Enraptured
Fear of Incest
The Heat of the Day
Her Private Hell
The Jealous and Free
Obsessed
The Outcasts
A Rage Within
Savage Surrender
The Soft Way
Three Women
The Third Sex
The Third Theme
The Unashamed
Veil of Torment
Whip of Desire

THE OUTCASTS

MARCH HASTINGS

CUTTING EDGE

ISBN-13: 978-1-952138-86-7

Published by
Cutting Edge Books
PO Box 8212
Calabasas, CA 91372
www.cuttingedgebooks.com

CHAPTER ONE

In the mirror, Jennie watched him cross the bedroom to stand beside her.

"I told you seven sharp," he said. "Why the hell aren't you dressed?"

She saw the red rims around his eyes and knew he had been drinking. All day probably, though he was still steady on his feet. She hated the smell of alcohol almost as much as she hated him. Glancing away, she picked up the comb and began to pull it through her hair.

Brian moved closer and she felt his big hand on her arm.

"Put that damned thing down and talk to me," he said.

He hadn't raised his voice. He didn't have to. The sharp points of his anger struck at her like darts thrown at a board. Sighing, she dropped the comb onto the dresser and turned around on the stool to face him.

His grip tightened as she moved. The fingertips dug into her arm.

She wasn't afraid of him. Just bored. She despised the fleeting look of fear in his blue eyes, the beads of perspiration along the bridge of his nose. At thirty, his face had already grown gaunt with deep lines of worry.

Still, she had married him, knowing what he was. And she had to live with him. There was no sense in aggravating him more than he had already aggravated himself. Tonight could be the most important night of his life. It could bring him recognition, favor. Perhaps even money.

As gently as she could, she loosened the grip of his fingers on her arm. "I'm almost ready," she said. "I just have to finish my make-up...."

"Well, get your face on and let's get the hell out of here." He stepped away from her and jabbed in his shirt pocket for a cigarette. "I told the Whitmans to be there by seven-thirty."

"I'm sure they will be," she said caustically. "At least, *she* will." She turned her back on him and leaned toward the mirror. The reflection of the flare from his cigarette lighter caught her eye. She watched him bring the lighter up to his cigarette. His hand trembled. For a moment, she allowed herself to bathe in a flood of self-satisfaction.

Brian walked away to the window and became absorbed in watching. Space, probably, she thought. He always stared at space. Or women. She picked up the lipstick brush and flicked the sable tip into position.

She had never met Leigh Whitman. Had never met any of the others, either, though well-meaning friends had kept her informed of Brian's activities. In the beginning, she hadn't really cared. All that had mattered then was that he stay away from her. Completely. A miserable pregnancy and a stillborn child had stifled in her any desire for sexual relations with him. The fear of becoming pregnant again had become a monster standing forever between them, forcing her to reject him time and time again. She had tried to explain to him that if he would only wait a little while, her terror would subside and she could be a wife to him as she had been before. Yet months had passed, long months of bitterness, of increasing drunkenness for Brian, before she would tolerate even his touch. And when finally she had wanted him, it was already too late.

Deftly, Jennie whielded the tiny brush, painting on the mouth that made her look seductive and attractive to all the world. She could have wept at the futility of it. Behind her, Brian puffed nervously on his cigarette and continued to stare morosely out the window. Sometimes she envied him his ability to concentrate with such absorption on total nothingness. She could never for a moment forget the aching throb of her loneliness, her need to be fondled and loved. But not by Brian. Not any more.

"There," she said finally, surveying the job she had just finished. Not bad, she thought. Not a gray hair to mar the smooth dark coils, not a wrinkle to tell the world how much she had suffered. She stood up and brushed crumbs of powder from the front of her dressing gown, then untied the sash and let the robe fall from her shoulders.

Brian stubbed out his cigarette on the brick ledge outside the window and tossed the butt into the street. "Which dress?"

"I thought the black one. With the emerald necklace."

He went to the closet and lifted the dress off its hanger. For a moment he glanced from the dress to Jennie and back again. He shook his head. "Not tonight," he said. He tossed the dress carelessly onto the single bed and turned back to the closet. Quickly he rifled through the long row of gowns. Lifting out a bright red silk, he held it toward her.

"But, Brian, in this weather ..." she started limply.

"In this weather," he said flatly. "I want you to look very special tonight."

"I'll look like a fool," she said sharply. "It must be ninety-five outside."

He jerked the dress toward her and she knew better than to argue with him further. She had always hated the dress. It was one of the many he had bought for her and brought home in the very early days of her pregnancy. It made her look like a whore, all breasts and behind and not much else. Yet he liked her best that way. When he liked her at all. And tonight he liked her because tonight he needed her.

She raised her arms and let him help her into the dress. Her muscles ached with fatigue and frustration. She felt the throb of a headache beginning to creep up from the back of her neck.

Brian slid the clasp up the long runners of the zipper and turned her around to face him.

She watched the glint of appreciation dart across his eyes. A film of perspiration clung to his upper lip. It had been a long time since he had looked at her like that. A long, long time. And she didn't want it now.

"You look pretty great," he said. The fingers of his right hand twitched nervously, as though wanting to touch and yet afraid to make the move.

"I'm glad," she said coldly. "I wouldn't want to disappoint your friend Mrs. Whitman."

He looked as though she had slapped him in the face. "Why the hell did you have to say that?" he rasped. "I meant for me, Jen. Remember me? The guy you married."

She heard the drunken whine creeping into his tone. Yet the outrage inside her would not lie still. "What a mistake that was," she said, plunging the knife of her words deep.

"You didn't think so five years ago," he whined. "You thought I was great then. Didn't you, Jen?"

She watched him take a step toward her and knew that he wanted her. Now. On the most important evening of his life. With a hundred people waiting for him. A half-hour late already. And he didn't give a damn about anything now but her. Not about anything.

And she didn't want him. She didn't want him. She didn't want him.

Over and over the words reeled across her brain. *I hate you, I hate you. I don't want you.* And yet even as she heard them, she knew the words were all lies. She felt herself beginning to relent, her knees going weak beneath her. As firmly as she could, she stepped back away from him.

"I was nineteen then," she said. She could hear the tremor in her own voice. "And you were an artist. With a beard." She smiled inwardly, almost fondly at the recollection of Brian's youthful shagginess. Yes, she had loved him then. Loved him desperately for the first three years of their marriage. And then ....

"You knew what you were doing," he said gently. "And if you loved me then, you could love me now. If you'd try just a little. We haven't changed all that much. Have we, Jen?"

A peculiar warmth had begun to spread through her. A feeling, not so much of desire for him, but of a desire for the past. The good days, before her pregnancy, before his unfaithfulness, his deceit and betrayal. And foolishly she wanted to trust him now, to believe the words he was saying to her, the promises he would in a moment make to her.

But still her pride would not let her give in to him. The humiliation, the pain she had suffered were too strong, too clear in her heart. She put her hand on his arm and held him away from her.

"You know why it happened," he said, his voice almost a whisper. "I would never have looked at another woman if you ...."

"Stop it, Brian," she said harshly. "I don't want to hear it. Don't you think I went through just as much as you did? If not more?"

"I know, baby," he crooned. "I know." His fingertips touched her arm, gently now, soothingly.

She shook off his touch. "You failed me when I needed you most," she said. "When I needed you to stand by me and help me get over ...." She could not speak the words. She could still not accept the reality of their dead son, of their dead love. Tears burned in her throat. Yet she turned from the comforting shoulder he offered her and stepped away from him.

He followed her. "I know I'm a bastard and a louse and all the other things you've called me in your head."

She leaned forward across the dressing table and gave her appearance a final check. She knew everything he was going to say. He had said it all before. Picking up the comb, she clicked her fingernails idly along the teeth. She braced herself for the onslaught of his words.

Brian stood close beside her. He made no attempt to touch her now, but she could feel his breath hot on the back of her neck. She wanted to turn and shove him away from her. She wanted to scream. She wanted to do anything to make him stop. And yet there was no stopping him.

"It's all in the past," he said. "I've told you that a million times. I haven't been near another woman for months."

"What about Mrs. Whitman?"

"Jesus Christ," he swore furiously. He spun away from her and stalked across the room and then back to her. "What the hell's the matter with you?" he said finally. "I'm trying to save this pile of crap you call a marriage and...."

"Why bother?" she said archly. "I think it's just fine the way it is. You do as you please and I'll do the same. You go play pottsy with Leigh Whitman and I'll find a little playmate for myself. That's what you want, isn't it?"

The disgust was bright in his eyes. "You know damned well it isn't," he breathed. "I want *you*, Jennifer. I always have."

"But it just so happens that Mrs. Whitman owns half interest in one of the best galleries in the city." She knew that she was being far more cruel than she needed to be. But she wanted him to squirm. Just a little. Like everything else about him lately, she hated him for this. "I remember," she went on, "when you had enough confidence in your work not to have to sleep with anybody in hopes of getting it shown."

"I've been trying to tell you for six months," he said, "that I'm not sleeping with Mrs. Whitman or anybody else. She likes my stuff and she's willing to help me."

Jennie snorted. "I'm sure she likes your stuff," she muttered.

"What?"

"Nothing," she said. She nearly screamed it. "Let me alone, Brian. Just let me alone." She blinked her eyes to clear away the tears threatening to spill over. Why did he have to taunt her so? Why did he have to lie to her? Everybody knew that he had been sleeping with that damned Leigh Whitman. Everybody. She'd heard it from a dozen sources.

"Jennie, look at me," Brian said roughly. He made a move toward her, then paused, as though reconsidering his action. "Look at me."

She turned her head away so that he could not see the tears. Never did she want him to know the pain he had caused her. She wanted him to believe only that she hated him as he must surely have hated her to have run out on her as he had. Yet in her heart she knew that it was not hate she felt, but only hurt and rage and frustration.

Gently, very gently, he put his fingertips on her chin and forced her to look at him.

"I love you, Jennifer," he whispered. "Why won't you let yourself believe that?"

Jennie swallowed hard to keep back the sob, but the sound of her anguish was loud between them. He moved in close to her then, taking her in his arms, cradling her against him like an infant. She felt herself relaxing and buried her face against the hard muscle of his chest.

His fingers stroked her hair, then trailed down to the side of her neck. He touched her with infinite tenderness, lulling her senses into a state of unreality. For a long moment she forgot the despair, the unhappiness that had taken over their lives. She closed her eyes and let her thoughts drift back in time, to the good days, the gentle days. The days and nights of love and laughter, and more love.

He had held her like this then. The first time they had lived through a thunder storm together. In a tiny motel cabin by the ocean, with the waves thundering in, banging up the beach almost as loud as the thunder rolling overhead. He had held her like this then. His hands had circled slowly on her back. Wooing her, lulling her, putting her into an hypnotic state.

And she felt his hands now, circling on her back as they had done then. And she could not separate the reality from the dreaming. He bent his head and his tongue trailed along the side of her neck and into her ear. Spasmodically she caught her breath and clung to him. His hands sought lower, cupped under her buttocks, pulling her close.

She felt the surge of his desire, sensed her own need rising to equal his. And she knew then that it was not the past, but the now. And that he had tricked her, had deceived her with the magic of his body against hers. She pulled herself up stiff and tried to break away from him.

Brian held her tight. His arm braced across her back, smashing her breasts flat against her chest.

"Not this time," he muttered. "If I have to rape you."

Jennie set her shoulders and struggled against him. "I hate you," she murmured. "I hate you."

She heard the metallic slide of a zipper. Felt him fumbling at the hem of her dress. She ducked her head forward suddenly and bit savagely at the side of his neck.

"God damn you." He grabbed hold of the slick red silk and yanked hard.

She tried to break away from him as the dress ripped off her. He grabbed her wrist with his free hand and twisted her arm up behind her back.

"I said, not this time, Jennie." He spun her to face him.

She realized too late that he was far drunker than she had imagined. Drunker and a lot more dangerous. The anger ebbed out of her and in its place rose fear. Never had she hated him so much. Yet good sense warned her not to fight him.

Brian flung her backward onto the bed and she did not try to resist. And then he was on top of her, his moist lips hunting hers greedily. His mouth mashed down against hers.

Jennie whimpered as her teeth cut into her lower lip. In pain and revolted by the savagery of his attack, she twisted sideways, trying to get away from his touch.

Brian ground himself into her. "I could kill you," he said against her ear.

He didn't bother to fumble with her panties. He grabbed them at the elastic and ripped them off as he had done with the dress.

Jennie groaned and turned her head away as far as she could. She began to count slowly, almost prayerfully.

Pain ripped through her. She bit hard on her lip and let the tears roll freely down her cheeks. Desperately, furiously, she fought him with a great inner resistance. She would not respond. There was no pleasure for her. And, after a while, not even pain.

He rolled away from her and lay on his back. His eyes focused on the ceiling, absorbed with nothingness.

She felt the slime of his sweat sticky across her stomach. Her legs ached from the force of his lust. She turned her head to look at him.

"I hope you're satisfied," she said.

Without answering, Brian sat up on the edge of the bed and ran his long fingers through his hair. The blonde strands had matted together with perspiration and when he took his hand away, long strands of hair fell across his forehead.

Jennie studied his face closely until she felt sure that all the fight had gone out of him. "You'd better be," she said then, "because you'll never do that again."

Brian grunted. When he looked at her, she saw that his eyes were bleary and bloodshot.

Without thinking about what she was going to say, Jennie launched into it. "I'm leaving you," she said. "God knows, I've got enough reason. Plenty of witnesses will back up the adultery bit and that's all I need in this state." She waited for a response, but when he said nothing, went on. "So you'd better hope

Mrs. Whitman will support you, because I can cost you a lot of alimony."

She finished her speech limply, all the steam knocked out of her by Brian's lack of response. She watched him narrowly, waiting for him to put up the arguments he always did when she threatened to walk out on him. How much he needed her, how he could never paint again without her.

Instead, Brian dug another cigarette out of his shirt pocket and lighted it. He stood up then and started toward the door. "You'd better put on some clothes," he said. "If you're coming."

"You sound as though you don't care."

"Frankly," he said, "I don't give a good Goddamn what you do."

Jennie watched him leave, listening to his footsteps click along the hall and down the stairs. Despite everything that had happened between them, this was the first time Brian had ever said that he no longer cared, and certainly the first time he had ever abused her physically. Yet, in her heart, she could not really blame him for what he had done. You could only drive a man so far, even a weakling like Brian. Then he would take no more. Remembering her repeated rejections during the past months, she was probably lucky that he hadn't murdered her.

Still, there was as much wrong on his side as on hers. If only he had stood by her, during those months of anguish, this wouldn't have happened now. She had been ready to love him, to be the wife he wanted.

She paused in the middle of a thought and remembered the last words she had flung at him. Divorce? No, she didn't want a divorce. She really didn't. She had said it in anger, rage, really.

Well, she didn't have time to think about it now. She wouldn't miss the opening for the world. Leigh Whitman would be there. And if she had any intention at all of saving the little that was left of her marriage, she'd better start sizing up the competition.

Not that she was sure, she reminded herself, that Brian was worth it. But if he was ....

Disgusted with herself and the incoherent whirl of her thoughts, Jennie jumped up from the bed and ran toward the bathroom, stripping off her bra as she moved.

CHAPTER TWO

N ew York steamed quietly in the August heat. The moment she left the air-conditioned comfort of their home on Bedford Street, Jennie felt her carefully groomed appearance begin to wilt. She touched fingertips to her hair, smoothing back an imaginary whisp. The smell of rotting garbage and the conglomerate sweat of the city's millions filled her nostrils. The throbbing in her temples took on a tom-tom beat.

Head high, heels clicking briskly along the concrete, she set off in the direction of Seventh Avenue, peering anxiously up the street for a cab. It was already eight-thirty, and although the delay had been Brian's fault, he would be angry that she had arrived so late.

At the corner she hailed a cab and directed the driver to an address on East Twelfth Street. Leaning back against the seat, she closed her eyes and turned her head toward the window, in no mood for chit chat with the cabbie.

Jennie knew that Brian would be stinking drunk by the time she reached the gallery. He always got that way when he had every reason to remain sober. If only she could avoid him all evening, she might be able to prevent a scene.

It seemed hardly likely. Her fingers tightened in her lap, anticipating the embarrassment of the evening. Around her, the Village crowds straggled along the streets, bent on finding a good time, yet too warm to hurry in search of it. A portrait painter sat in the center of a street-corner gathering, with his charcoal rejuvenating the old and beautifying the homely. It was all a scene she knew intimately and loved, yet now she saw nothing of it. The cab stopped for a light. A grimy old man selling flutes for a quarter leaned through the window and tootled almost into her ear. She barely noticed. All of her stretched forward, up the blocks to the gallery, anxious to be there, more anxious for the evening to end.

At Twelfth Street the cab sped east toward Third Avenue. As it pulled to a stop along the curb, Jennie fumbled in her purse and handed the driver a bill. She watched the cab disappear up the street before she turned to face the gallery.

A renovated store at street level, the gallery stood tucked in between a warehouse and a second-hand book store. Behind its plate-glass window, a small, hand-lettered placard announced the opening tonight of an exhibit of the works of Brian Dunbar, noted Village artist. Inside she could see perhaps fifty people, milling like cattle between the whitewashed brick walls in a space meant for half the number. From where she stood, no one seemed to be paying the least attention to either the art or the artist. Champagne glasses and cigarettes waved animatedly and she could hear the din of conversation and an occasional laugh.

Gathering all her strength, Jennie stepped forward and shoved open the warped wooden door. For a moment she paused just inside, searching through the crowd for a glimpse of Brian. No one came forward to greet her. Glancing at faces, Jennie realized that she knew hardly anyone in the room. Most of them, she had been told, were friends of the Whitmans, invited by Leigh to appreciate the new talent she had discovered. One or two at least would be reviewers. Few of them would be friends of Brian's or herself. No surprise, considering the state of their marriage. They rarely went anywhere together anymore. No one came to visit.

Jennie sighed and stepped into the fray. She had no idea where Brian might be hiding. At the moment, it was almost a relief not to know, for it was obvious from the snatches of conversation she caught that Brian Dunbar, noted Village artist, had not set the art world on fire. Moving slowly among the gossipers, stopping now and then for a brief word, Jennie made a casual survey of the collection as it had been presented for the crowd to see. She knew them all, the sweat and the love that had gone into them. Nudes, mostly. Modern madonnas and muscular young men. Sex on a rampage, unrequited passion splattered across canvas for all the world to see. But a sick, distorted passion, reeking of anguish and fear and hatred. In Brian's hands, sex became no longer a symbol of joy and regeneration, but the symbol of the world's destruction.

She felt the touch of cool fingers on her elbow and involuntarily started. Turning quickly, she found herself smiling into the chubby, good-natured face of Jake Potter, Brian's one real friend.

"Hello, Jake," she said, giving him a quick peck on the lips.

"Fine time for you to show up," he chided. "Where the hell have you been?"

She tried to avoid meeting his eyes, a neat trick, since they were exactly on a level with her own. "I ... I was delayed," she said limply. "Where's Brian?"

Jake grinned. "Probably piled up in a corner somewhere. You know Brian. He was lit when he got here. And then ...." He raised the champagne glass in his right hand and swung it toward her. "Want a drink?"

"No thanks," she said quickly. The one thing she didn't need in her life now was a hangover. "How has it been going, Jake?"

Jake's grin widened. "Great. Just great."

Jennie had always known that he was a lousy liar. No matter how hard he tried, he couldn't cover up the sadness in his soft amber eyes. "No, Jake," she said gently. "I mean, really, how is it going?"

Jake shrugged and took a sip of his drink. "It stinks," he said flatly. "But what the hell do you expect?" He glared at her defiantly. "These rich bastards don't know art when they see it." He waved his arm in a wide circle and the champagne slopped over the side of the glass. "They're a bunch of pigs, you know that."

Jennie smiled. "I also know they're the ones who can afford to buy paintings," she said. She turned then and ran her glance quickly along the canvases lining the far wall. Her nose wrinkled ever so slightly. "They're not very good, are they?"

Jake followed the line of her glance. He looked very tired. "Not anymore," he said. "Five years ago, yes. He had it then. But ...." he shrugged. "Something happened."

She nodded. "Um hum. He married me."

"I didn't say that," Jake said defensively.

"You didn't have to. I know it myself."

She paused a moment to say hello to a face she remembered vaguely from somewhere. "We've had a lot of trouble," she went on, turning back to Jake. "You know. The baby and everything. I don't have to tell you, Jake. You've been the one friend we've had through all this."

"Yeah," Jake grunted, "I know."

She watched him raise the glass for another sip and the way the light reflected off the soft red fuzz on the back of his hand. "I suppose this will ruin his chance for a showing at the Whitmans' gallery," she said slowly. She had meant it to sound like a statement. Yet a faint tinge of hope lilted her words into a question.

Jake laughed shortly. "Oh, I wouldn't say that."

Something about the tone of his voice riveted her attention. "I don't understand."

Jake nodded toward a tall, beautifully dressed woman at the far side of the room. "She's the only one with sense enough to realize the boy's got talent."

Jennie did not even hear his words. She had become absorbed in the minute scrutiny of the woman who had become her competition. A woman in her early forties with short-cropped pepper and salt hair and the most gorgeous profile—from end to end— that Jennie had ever seen in her life. Leigh Whitman was a competitor worthy of careful consideration. Tall, slender and every inch a woman, she had gathered around herself now a group of the youngest and most handsome men in the place. Jennie noticed their faces, all of them held in rapt attention, all of them eager and enchanted. Whatever Leigh Whitman had, any woman would have given her right arm for it—including Jennie. But at the moment, Jennie concerned herself with only one thing: how the devil would she win Brian back from this stunning creature?

And speaking of Brian .... Once more she made a hasty survey of the faces hovered around Mrs. Whitman. Brian was not there. Relieved at least for this small favor, she started to turn her attention once more to Jake when she noticed Mrs. Whitman take leave of her admirers and make her way toward them.

"She's coming over here," Jennie breathed, startled into a kind of terror at the thought of facing the enemy at such close range.

"Why not?" Jake said.

Jennie couldn't think of an answer. Instead, she stood frozen to the spot as Leigh Whitman approached and extended her hand.

"You're Jennifer," Mrs. Whitman said.

Jennie could not identify the trace of accent that tinged the words. It sounded like a combination of many tongues from many lands and lent an air of mystery to the serene face and deep-green eyes.

Smiling stiffly, Jennie accepted the outstretched hand. "And you're Leigh. I've heard so much about you from my husband." She tried to keep her tone light, tried not to hint at the resentment she bore this woman. But she felt the weight of her jealousy and fear heavy on her tongue.

If Leigh noticed her discomfort, she gave no indication. She merely turned to Jake and handed him her empty glass. "Be a dear, will you?" she said.

"Yes, ma'am," Jake said eagerly. He went off quickly through the crowd.

Jennie watched him go, almost hating him for his eagerness. Even Jake, the perennial bachelor, running like a hound after a bitch in heat.

"What are you thinking?" Leigh's deep voice interrupted her thoughts.

Startled, Jennie averted her glance. "I was thinking that you certainly know how to handle men."

Leigh laughed deep in her throat. "And is it so difficult for you?" she said. Her eyes roamed slowly over Jennie's tight-packed gown, then back to her face. "I think you have all that's required."

Flushing with confusion, Jennie tried to answer and found the words stuck in her throat. Instinctively she knew that she could never get the better of this woman in any way. There was something about her strangely challenging, disquieting. For all she tried, Jennie found herself speechless and terribly ill at ease.

Still oblivious of Jennie's confusion, Leigh continued. "After all, men are only little boys with long tails. And little boys are no problem at all." She flashed a smile that seemed to brighten the whole room. But her attention was for Jennie alone.

"I suppose you're right," Jennie managed, unable to apply any thought to the conversation at hand. All she wanted in the world was to get away from the woman, have a chance to think, to make plans—if she could think that clearly. For obviously she could not simply dismiss the woman as a rival for her husband.

And speaking of husbands.... "Did Mr. Whitman come with you?" Jennie asked suddenly. Then, facetiously, she could not resist adding, "I've never heard my husband speak about Mr. Whitman."

The woman laughed easily. "Dirk? I couldn't drag him to one of these affairs." She put her hand lightly on Jennie's wrist. "I suppose you have the same thing with Brian. Dirk's a bit of a fanatic in his own way. He's got a collection of antique cars and nothing, but nothing can take him away from them."

"Except you," Jennie put in.

For the first time, the woman's composure cracked just slightly around the edges. Well, maybe not cracked, Jennie decided. But definitely chipped a little. So there was something not quite perfect about this splendid and apparently complete creature. Whatever it might be, Jennie determined, she would find it out. And somehow she would use it, use it to ruin the woman and get her forever out of their lives. Brian could make a name for himself without Leigh Whitman's help. And if he couldn't——

The fingers tightened on Jennie's wrist. "Not all marriages are as successful as yours," Leigh said quietly.

Jennie stared at her stupidly. The woman's tone had sounded completely honest. Yet how could she call her marriage to Brian a success? How could anyone who knew either one of them?

Jennie opened her lips to speak, but was saved the necessity by the reappearance of Jake.

"Here you go, Mrs. Whitman." He handed over the glass with a bow that, for Jake, was quite courtly.

Mrs. Whitman released her hold on Jennie's arm and accepted the drink. "Thank you, Jake," she said, giving him a smile as radiant as the one she had lavished on Jennie only moments before.

He's blushing, Jennie realized. Even I fluster him. Poor Jake, he couldn't possibly know how to deal with a creature like this.

Gently, she took Jake's hand and linked her fingers with his. She could feel the heat of his palm burning against her own. "You didn't happen to fall over Brian, did you?"

Jake blinked his appreciation. "He's asleep on a chair back in the corner," he said. "Over there by the punch table." He nodded in the general direction of the back of the room.

"Oh, yes," Mrs. Whitman said. "I almost forgot what I came over to say. I've invited you two out to Oyster Bay for the weekend." She tilted her head slightly and smiled down into Jennie's eyes. "Brian accepted, but I'm not at all sure he'll remember by morning."

The last place in the world Jennie wanted to spend any weekend was in Leigh Whitman's house. "Well, I ...." She hesitated, feeling Jake's urgent signal through his trembling hand. She glanced at him quickly. The message in his eyes was clear. "... I'd be delighted," she finished. "When will you be expecting us?"

"Friday evening," Leigh said. "Early. Brian knows the way."

In spite of her own insecurity in the situation, Jennie did not have the feeling that Mrs. Whitman was being snide. And for just a moment, she had a flicker of doubt concerning the rumors she had heard about Brian and his patroness. Still, when a woman looked like Leigh Whitman, a husband would have to be a little queer not to be tempted. Anyhow, thinking about it wouldn't help a thing. They'd take this little trip this weekend. And she'd know soon enough for herself.

Jake nudged her and Jennie realized that Mrs. Whitman was waiting calmly for a reply. "Of course," she said quickly. "We'll see you then. Friday evening. Early."

"Fine," Leigh said heartily. "I think you'll like Oyster Bay." She paused and the green eyes darkened. "And I hope you'll like us."

She smiled then and was gone, swallowed up quickly in the circle of young men waiting eagerly for her return.

"Well?" Jake drawled beside her.

"Well what?" Jennie snapped.

"What do you think of the lady?"

Jennie bit back the flow of nasty words on the tip of her tongue. No reason why she should spill out her fears to Jake. He'd only laugh and call her a jealous cat. Which she was and she didn't need to hear it from him.

"I think she's charming," she said. "No wonder Brian's so attentive to her most of the time."

Jake shook his head. "You got it all wrong, kid," he said quietly. "She's got a couple of dozen guys dancing on her string. But not the way you think. She likes company and they're tryin' to con a fast buck. Most of 'em never get a cent out of her. But right now she likes Brian, real well. And he needs her, Jen. That's why ...." He shrugged.

"That's why I have to spend the weekend at Oyster Bay with her and her nutty husband."

Jake grinned. "He's not so nutty. He's got her and more money than the U. S. mint."

Despite his good cheer, Jennie could find little encouragement in Jake's words. It was possible, maybe, that Brian spent five or six hours a day with the woman—every day—and had never gone to bed with her. Possible. Maybe. But even so, a cozy weekend at the beach would change all that. Even with her husband lurking down in the garage.

A thought struck Jennie that almost amused her. She wondered if she had been invited along to lure Dirk out of sight and leave Brian alone with——

The sound of shattering glass brought an abrupt end to her thinking. Automatically, her attention shifted to the back end of the long room, where Brian had been sleeping.

In the sudden, awful stillness of the room, Jennie knew that her instinct had been right. Through a forest of legs, she saw her husband, sprawled on his face in the debris of the broken punch bowl. For a long moment, no one moved. Suddenly Brian let out a bellow like the mating cry of a bull ape and the crowd closed in around him.

Dragging Jennie by the hand, Jake shoved his way toward Brian's prostrate form. Elbows dug into her and a thin, pointed heel cut sharply into her instep. She swore inwardly, but kept the shadow of a smile pasted across her lips.

They joined the semicircle of craning necks peering down at him. No one stepped forward to help. A woman kept saying, "He tried to pick it up. He was going to throw it."

Jake let go of her hand and went to kneel beside his friend. Jennie watched him pull a handkerchief out of his back pocket and dab at a cut on Brian's chin. At the sight of blood, even the shadow of her smile faded. Quickly she moved in beside Jake.

She looked down at the bloated face, the alcohol-soaked body of her husband. Revulsion and disgust choked up in her throat. Yet she was all wife now, ready to defend him, fight for him, die for him. She could tell him later her private opinion.

"Is he all right, Jake?" She kept her voice low, yet loud enough to quiet the chattering around them.

The crowd pressed closer. Jennie felt them closing in, like vultures at a feast. She hated every damned one of their shiny, disgusting faces. She hated them and she wanted desperately to tell them so. But she bent closer over her now unconscious husband. Her hand moved to caress his forehead.

"Nothing a bath won't cure," Jake said, but loudly, hating the vultures as much as she and not caring if they knew it. "We'd better get him out of here."

A pair of legs broke clear of the forest. "I'll drive you."

Jennie recognized Mrs. Whitman's voice. She wanted to tell the woman she could drop dead for all any of them cared. She wanted to tell her to take her damned gallery and— But instead, she turned to smile up at the woman.

"That's very kind of you," she said. The sweetness cloyed in her mouth.

"I'll go bring the car around front," Leigh said. "I had to park halfway to Brooklyn." She didn't wait for an answer. Ignoring the peering faces and the questions, she made her way briskly through the curious onlookers and to the door.

Jennie glanced across at Jake. "Well?"

He reached out to pat her hand. "You played it beautifully," he said. "I couldn't have written the scene better myself."

Jennie helped him roll Brian onto his back. The front of the white silk shirt was torn and stained, but there was no sign of blood nor of damage to Brian himself.

"God protects drunks and fools," Jake murmured. "And, boy, you're both."

He waved a hand for assistance and two men stepped forward. Jake took most of Brian's six-three hugeness on his own back. The vultures moved aside to let him through.

Jennie watched the crowd. Some of them shocked, some of them repelled, most of them simply amused. Stupid, stupid people. Stupid, stupid people with their money. Noses in the air like they smelled a pile of crap. They didn't even deserve one of Brian's paintings.

Not that she'd have to worry about that.

The faces swung back toward her and she no longer saw them as faces. Through the mist of her tears, she saw nothing but the futility and the pain. He was ruined. He had ruined himself, as an artist and as a man. Not all by himself. No. She'd done more than her share.

She shook the thoughts away from her. No time now for regret, for self pity. She could hate Brian all she wanted to. But it was herself that she hated more. The time had come to start righting a few wrongs in their life.

She took a deep breath and pulled her chin high. Then, without glancing to either side, she stepped forward and followed Jake's squat figure toward the gallery door.

CHAPTER THREE

Jennie set the coffee pot on the kitchen table and pulled out a wrought-iron chair. A faint breeze drifted in on the midnight air, the first breeze in weeks that had even stirred the filmy curtains. She tugged at the window to let in whatever breeze she could find. The window stuck in its frame.

Sighing, she gave up the attempt and slumped down in the chair. Even the house seemed against her tonight. This lovely old house, only ten feet wide and three stories high, that they had bought for almost nothing and put together with their own hands. She laughed. The windows didn't work, the plumbing leaked, the doors sagged. What did an artist and a beautician know about putting together a house? Or about anything, it seemed.

She listened to the drip of the coffeepot, a sound that usually meant warmth, a lift of sagging spirits. Tonight it grated on her nerves till she felt she might scream. She folded her arms on the table and pressed her forehead against the warm flesh.

They couldn't go on like this. This way, they weren't *going* anywhere. Brian was drinking himself straight into the grave. And she? She was probably in worse shape than he was. Nervous as a cat. Filled with hate ... for everything. Nothing pleased her anymore. Nothing. Somewhere in her heart she loved him as much as she ever had and she believed that he was the same way. But too much had happened between them. Too much that neither could forgive, or forget. Too many petty fights, too many misunderstandings and too little consideration.

Even Jake had said that Brian was better off before he married her. He had been good then. His work had meant something. He had sold, gained a certain recognition. But not anymore. Artistically, he was already dead. And she had done it to him.

She heard the sound of Jake's footsteps coming heavily down the front stairs. She wanted to relax and smile for him. She tried, but she couldn't make it. The worry lines etched tiredly around her mouth.

Jake glanced at her, then reached for the coffeepot. He poured for both of them. "He's asleep," he said. "I got him cleaned up as much as I could."

She watched him pull out a chair and sit down. The delicate chair looked foolishly small beneath him. She tipped cream into her cup, then a mound of sugar, her movements slow and mea-sured. "He's finished, isn't he?" she said finally.

Jake snorted. "Well, he sure as hell did his best to be," he said. He took a long drink of the hot coffee. "But I wouldn't worry too much, if I were you. Mrs. Whitman still seems to be on his side."

"Oh, she gives me a pain," Jennie snapped.

Jake laughed. "So I've gathered. And damned if I know what special charm Brian has for her. The condition he's in, I don't know why a woman would even look at him." He glanced up quickly. "I don't mean you," he said. "You're in love with the guy."

Jennie sighed. "Don't be so sure," she said.

"Ah, come off it, Jen. You know you've got a thing for Brian. God knows, I wish sometimes you didn't. I think you could do better for yourself."

She looked at him sharply. "I thought you were Brian's best friend."

"Yeah. Sure. I love the guy, too. But that doesn't mean I don't know what a bastard he can be." He put his big hand over hers. "I always did think he gave you a rotten deal after the baby died."

She heard the genuine concern in his tone and her heart warmed toward him. No one else had ever known how Brian's infidelity had hurt her then. She had never mentioned it to Jake, yet he had known, as he always knew everything. "Well, it doesn't matter anymore, Jake," she said. "I'm leaving him."

Jake stared at her blankly.

"That's what I said, I'm leaving him," she repeated.

"I don't believe it," he said flatly.

She pulled away from his hand and turned sideways in the chair, away from his probing eyes. "I have to," she went on. "I'm killing him this way. We ... we have nothing together anymore. You know that. No understanding. No love. No ...." She hesitated self-consciously.

"No sex," Jake finished for her.

"Well, almost," she admitted. "Something happened tonight before the opening .... Oh, I don't want to talk about it, Jake. It doesn't make any difference, I tell you. I've just had enough. And I'm sure Brian has, too."

"Yeah?"

"Yes. He told me so tonight."

Jake shook his head, slowly and ponderously. "I still don't believe it," he said. "But if you do mean it, well ... I'll do whatever I can to help."

She smiled warmly. "Thanks, Jake. But I think Brian will need help more than I will."

"If you think that, then you'd better stay with him."

Jennie had no answer, as she never had an answer when she really needed one. She blinked at him helplessly, wanting him to answer for her, wanting him to tell her that whatever she did would be the right thing. Somebody had to feel that way about her. Somebody.

"Look," he said after a while, "I'm not going to tell you to go. I like you both too much. But if you do ...." He shrugged.

"You'll understand?"

"Understand, sure," he said. He looked down at his cup, apparently absorbed in studying its contents. "I'll even marry you, if nobody else'll have you."

She had known Jake too long to misunderstand his words. Yet it shocked her to hear them. She had never thought of Jake in love with anyone, let alone herself, and she didn't want to think about it now. She had too much else to ponder, too many problems already.

"When you have time, think about it," he went on. "I don't expect you to answer me now."

"Jake, I. ... I don't know what to say. I ... ."

"Don't say anything, Jen," he said. "Not now." For a moment he gazed at her intently. Then, suddenly, he burst out laughing.

The sound of his laughter infuriated her. How could he possibly laugh when she was so confused and unhappy?

"What's so damned funny?" she snapped.

"We are," he said. "You know, if I wrote this dialogue into one of my plays, I'd get hooted off the stage."

She saw his point. But she was too close to tears to risk a good laugh. "This isn't a play," she said sharply. "It happens to be my life, corny as it is."

He pushed back his chair and got up. "It happens to be my life, too," he said quietly. "And that's why I'm laughing, Jen. Because I might cry otherwise."

The sudden dead seriousness of his tone made her uneasy. She knew what was coming next. Jake was, after all, a man. Just a boy with a long tail, as Mrs. Whitman called it. But that long tail made a hell of a difference.

She watched him narrowly, standing there leaning toward her, his face all wrinkled with nervousness, his reddish crewcut bristling, glinting in the light. And she waited, a little afraid, not wanting to hurt him.

"I know I'm not much to look at," he said. "I mean, I'm fat and getting a little bald and my behind's pretty close to the ground. I guess you could do a lot better than me."

She wanted to say something, anything to stop him. Anything to save him the embarrassment of rejection. Yet even now she could not hurt him, could not speak the words.

"But I'd be good to you, Jen," he went on. "And I can take care of you. I'm making good money now, with this television stuff. I'd give you a nice home."

"I know that, Jake," she said gently. She had to say it now, before it was too late. Even more gently, she went on. "You're the dearest friend I have in all the world, Jake. The only friend, really. And I love you as a friend. But—"

"But not as a lover," he interrupted. He shook his head. "You know, we're still doing this corny bit with the dialogue. Why the hell don't we act like a couple of sharp kids from the twentieth century?"

"What do you mean?" she said innocently, thrown completely off-guard by his change of tactics.

He shrugged and his big hands raised in a gesture that rendered her innocence foolish. "You know what I mean," he said simply. "I'm hung up on you, Jen. I always have been. I guess that's what it means to be in love with somebody. Anyhow," he sighed, "I want you any way I can get you. Even if I have to marry you."

Jennie's right eyebrow arched with amusement.

"Yeah," he said. "Even if. And that's more than I've ever done for any other dame."

Jennie picked up her cup. The coffee was cold now with a scum of cream across the top. She didn't want it, but she drank it down. When she could face him, she lowered the cup.

"Well, I guess I should thank you at least for being honest," she said. "I don't suppose it would do me any good to act the part of outraged innocence?"

"Hell, no," Jake said bluntly. "I mean, I know you haven't fooled around since you've been married. I guess you think maybe Brian's done enough for the both of you."

Without realizing it, Jake had confirmed all the rumors she had heard, had made a lie of all Brian's protestations to the contrary. Until tonight Jake had never said a word about Brian's activities. But he had known. He must have known everything.

"Go on," she said calmly.

"Well, what the hell do I have to do, draw pictures?" he said. A tinge of annoyance touched his words. "You said you're leaving him. So if you're leaving him, you need a place to go." He shrugged. "So you might as well shack up at my place."

Jennie laughed lightly. "That's what I've always liked about you, Jake. No starry-eyed romance with you. Everything spelled out neatly in four letter words."

"You got anyplace better to go?" he asked levelly.

She stared at him for a moment, not seeing Jake, the man she had called her friend, but a stranger. Jake, who had been gentle, considerate, always willing to help. And maybe you could say that's what he was doing now. Helping. In his own clumsy way. But he'd sure picked a hell of a time for it. How could she tell him she needed to be alone, to think, to plan? How could she make him understand that she needed someone to love her, not just a body beside her in bed?

But maybe he would love her. Maybe he would. And God knew, she needed somebody. Without Brian ....

Without Brian was something she didn't want to think about. Not yet. Not for a long, long time. Maybe someday, she would be able to think about him, about them. But now, she needed to forget. Needed to lose herself in the arms of another man. Needed to find herself through a man's love.

She knew she would never love Jake. Not that way. And yet .... He was a man. And he wanted her. She was in a hell of a position to be choosy.

She pushed her chair away from the table. The breeze from the partly-open window touched the back of her neck soothingly. Somewhere in the distance she heard the rumble of thunder above the flow of late traffic. People going home. Home to love, to sleep. And she? Where did she have to go?

"Well?" Jake said.

Jennie stood up slowly and held out her hand. "Well, like you say, Jake. What the hell. Where else have I got to go?"

He took her hand and stepped back to look at her. His eyes probed at her closely, stripping away her clothes, searching into every pore of her.

Jennie felt her stomach convulse with revulsion. She had never seen Jake like this before. His eyes narrowed with lust, his face red, his neck bulging against the tight collar. She felt like a pig on a platter. And she hated him, hated him, hated him.

Yet she had offered herself.

He pulled her to him suddenly and kissed her full on the mouth, his tongue going deep against hers. He gripped her buttocks and pressed himself hard against her. She felt the rise of his passion.

Suddenly she could not go through with it. She put her hand against his chest and tried to shove him away. "For God's sake," she said, "not here."

Jake held her tight. "Why the hell not? Who's gonna know?"

"Brian."

His mouth mashed down on hers, choking off her words. She felt herself being lifted, carried toward the living room. His tongue moved against her lips. She gagged.

He got her onto the couch and dropped to his knees beside her. "Don't give me a hard time," he whispered. "You want it as much as I do."

His hand inched up the inside of her thigh. And then he was cupping his hand against her, circling slowly.

She felt her body catch fire, the warmth spreading upward and outward, reaching into every part of her. And she knew that he was right. She wanted it as much as he did. Every bit as much. And she didn't care if it was Jake or Brian or a chimpanzee. Two years...two years.... Her love-starved body screamed out to him. Her back arched and she welcomed him.

And it was good. So good. She met the force of his passion, urging him on. Not wanting to let him go...not wanting ever to let him go.

And when it happened, she clung to him desperately, clutching him to her with her knees, holding him, holding him....

She lay beside him on the couch, her hand touching him, still wanting him. It had been perfect, for the brief instant it lasted. Perfect, yet she felt as though her appetite had been only whetted. Maybe there wasn't enough in the world to satiate the lust raging through her. Maybe no man could do it. Maybe there would always be this emptiness, this need that no one could fill.

Jake sighed and licked his lips.

She hadn't remembered till then that it was Jake beside her. She hadn't wanted to think about that. But she had to face it now. She turned her head to look at him.

He lay on his back with his eyes closed and a schoolboy grin on his face. A smirk. She wanted to take the damned smirk and shove it down his throat. Yet she couldn't blame him. Not for what had happened, surely. She had wanted him to. She realized suddenly she had been wanting someone to for a hell of a long time. Jake just happened to be the first one who asked. But he wouldn't be the last, of that she would make sure.

Jennie touched his lips with her finger.

He kissed her finger and made a grab for it with his lips.

"Huh uh," she said. "Next time."

He opened his eyes and looked up at her. "You mean that?" he said.

"What?"

"Next time?"

Jennie sighed. "Why not?"

Jake sat up, the self-satisfied grin still plastered across his face. "Yeah," he said. "Why not?" He patted himself. "Nothin' like—"

"Don't get any grandiose ideas," Jennie said sharply. "I need you, I admit that. But you haven't got any exclusive rights to the property."

"Let me worry about that," Jake said. "All a woman needs is a good man to keep her in line."

Jennie laughed. "And you're the man?"

"Yeah," Jake said. "I'm the man who can do it."

Jennie stood up and smoothed down the front of her dress. Let him think what he wanted, she decided. He wouldn't get in her way. Nothing could. She was even with Brian now. And before she got finished, she'd make Brian look like a saint.

CHAPTER FOUR

Jennie awoke at noon. For a moment she lay still, listening for a sound of movement from Brian's room. Hearing nothing but silence, she breathed a sigh of relief. She had a lot of thinking to do before she was ready to face Brian. Thinking … and planning. Despite Jake's offer to support her, she realized that she would be better off finding herself a job. A place of her own to live.

She swung her feet over the side of the bed and stood up and stretched luxuriously. She felt wonderful, just wonderful. All of her relaxed, the tension gone out of her back and thighs. Funny, what a difference a little physical satisfaction could make to the whole being. But really, not funny at all. How easily she could become a slave to her desire, letting Jake and others like him possess her, use her, demanding and wanting nothing in return but the pleasure of the moment.

If only Brian had understood and tried to help her when she needed him most. When, for months, her body had yearned for fulfillment and her mind had screamed in terror.

The memory of her suffering rushed in on her and she shuddered involuntarily. How could any man understand what she had been through? The terrible, terrible longing for love, to create a child as a product of that love. And the equally terrible dread of losing another child. It was a fear she hadn't been able to stare down. A demon that stalked her constantly, turning desire to revulsion, love to hatred.

Jennie sighed and pattered barefoot into the bathroom. Her face in the mirror over the sink looked tired and drawn. Quickly, she brushed her teeth and rinsed. Jake had promised to be back by one with the *Times,* and himself. A lousy review, if any, for Brian, and for her ....

Realistically, Jennie accepted the fact that she wanted him for that. She didn't give a damn about Jake. Not really. And she was realistic enough to admit that, too.

In the bedroom, she chose a white silk shirt and a pair of slacks tight enough to keep Jake around as long as she wanted him. She checked her behind in the mirror and realized that she had put on a few pounds. She liked the added fulness of her figure and she smoothed her hand over her rump, knowing that Jake would not be the only man in her life.

She didn't even think about Brian that way now. Though he was certainly better than Jake. But, except for the weekend, she was finished with Brian, for good. As a final act of loyalty, she and Jake had agreed that she stay with Brian till after the visit with the Whitmans for the sake of appearances. After last night's fiasco, Brian would need all the help he could get.

Smoothing the heavy mass of her hair back from her forehead, Jennie caught it with a clasp and fastened it tight at the base of her skull. She pinched her cheeks deftly for a dash of natural color. Without make-up, she looked sixteen and innocent. Not that she expected anyone to be fooled by the appearance. But it was good for her morale.

She stepped into the hall and moved cautiously along toward Brian's room. The odor of alcohol hung heavy in the stagnant air. She inched the window up halfway, careful not to make a sound.

Brian grunted and rolled over.

Jennie held her breath. When he was quiet once more, she leaned over the bed and surveyed the sleep-swollen face. The cut on his chin had closed up, she noticed, hardly visible now through the morning bristle. The skin of his cheeks looked pasty and there were sick, blue rings under his eyes. Even in sleep, his fists were clenched, as though to fend off an unfriendly world.

Well, he could stop fighting, Jennie thought. A few more days and it would all be over. He'd probably let his beard grow and move back to a loft. He'd be happier that way, just as she would be happier. She hoped.

Quietly, she closed the bedroom door behind her and went quickly down the stairs and out to the kitchen. The sun glinted hotly through the dusty panes. The tiny room smelled airless and suffocating. She opened the back door to let in the morning air and switched on the small fan by the sink.

She never ate breakfast, even at noon. A cup of hot coffee and a couple of aspirin; orange juice sometimes for a chaser. She made herself a cup of instant with hot water from the tap and drank it straight. Then she set the tea kettle up to boil.

She leaned back against the sink and lit a cigarette from a crumpled pack on the cupboard. She didn't smoke, really. Brian always said she fumed. And she was fuming now.

It wasn't so much that she had anything against Jake, but a girl had to look out for her own interests. She was damned bored with being poor. Oh, they managed all right, if you called pinching pennies managing. But they were in hock up to their ears. The house was mortgaged and they had even borrowed on the insurance. A girl likes a new dress once in a while. And Jennie was tired of mending seams.

Jake would do for a starter. And then—

The front door chime sang through the house. Jennie glanced at the pussy-cat clock. Not quite quarter of one. But it would be Jake, she knew. Impatient, anxious to possess her, to assert the manhood he had promised her. She sighed. Poor Jake.

She doused her cigarette at the sink and went out quickly to the foyer. Hesitating, she set a smile across her features, hoping it looked for real.

Jake stepped back and took a long look. He didn't whistle, but she got the message.

He took a folded newspaper from beneath his arm. "Not a word," he said. "Not even an announcement."

Jennie stepped aside and closed the door behind him. "I suppose it's just as well," she said. "Not even his dear Mrs. Whitman could have been impressed after last night."

"Ah, come on," Jake said. "Some of his stuff isn't so bad. He'll get a Sunday review. They're the only ones that count anyhow."

Jennie went into the living room, with Jake trailing after her. With her fingertips, she brushed a film of dust from the top of the coffee table. "I hate this weather," she said. "Everything gets so dirty."

"Yeah," Jake breathed. He moved in close behind her.

Jennie felt his hands on her hips, felt him press himself against her from behind.

"You don't waste any time," she said.

"What the hell for?" Jake grinned. "I waited all night already."

Jennie took his hands gently with her own and lifted them away from her. "Brian might wake up," she said. "I don't want to make a scene, Jake." She turned to face him. "You understand, don't you?"

"Yeah, sure," Jake said. "Brian. I been waiting five years for him to climb out of your bed, Jen." He put his hands on her shoulders now and pulled her toward him. "I'm tired of waiting."

The backs of her knees touched the edge of the couch. His hands moved around to her back, circling slowly. Moving lower. His fingers toyed with the button of her slacks.

Her hand clasped over his on the button. She shook her head violently. She opened her mouth to speak.

Jake's mouth came down hard on hers. His tongue probed between her lips.

The fight went out of her. She let herself relax against him, let his hands search over her body. Her senses began to spin.

Without the awareness of motion, she was on the couch. Fingers of air teased at her skin. Her back arched eagerly, hungrily, pleading with him to hurry.

Jake knelt beside her and buried his face in her belly. "Jesus," he whispered. "Jesus." His lips trailed along her ribs, burning a path of desire. His mouth moved eagerly, tantalizing, promising.

Torturously slow, he played her body. The pain of expectancy was exquisite, yet unbearable. She needed him, needed him, needed him to hurry.

She grabbed at the bristles of his crew cut, her fingers working convulsively. "Please," she moaned "Please."

Jake moved beside her on the couch. "We got all day," he said. He took her hand in his and drew it to him, leading her touch.

It's crazy, she thought, how I need him. How I need him. Now.

She rolled over on him, pressing herself tight against him.

Jake sighed. "That's the way I like it, baby," he said. "Just like that."

Desire raged through her. Furiously she worked herself against him, wanting him, all of him. Inside her head a siren screamed, its harsh voice tearing through her brain.

She felt herself lurching toward completion.

Jake grunted and she knew he had had enough.

"Damn you," she murmured. "Damn you, damn you."

But it was no good. She felt the strength go out of him. Disgusted, enraged with her frustration, she rolled away from him. She closed her eyes.

After a long time, Jake touched her arm. "Look," he said, "I'm sorry."

She heard the apology, the hurt in his tone. And she loathed him. Loathed herself, for letting it happen. "It's not your fault," she said. "You tried."

"Yeah," Jake said. He got up, fixing his trousers. He kept his glance averted, apparently unable to face the disgust in her eyes. "I guess I'll be going." He hesitated.

She knew he wanted her to ask him to stay. Knew that in failing her, he had failed himself. Yet she could not bring herself to say the words that would save him.

"Yes," she said. "I guess you'd better." She stood up beside him.

"Never mind," Jake said. "I know where the door is."

She watched him go. He looked older, somehow, more slumped and baggy than she had ever seen him before. And for a moment she pitied him.

But only for a moment.

From the kitchen she heard the hiss of water boiling out of the kettle and onto the stove. Disorientated by her experience with Jake, it took her several moments to realize the source of the sound.

"Turn the goddamned thing off," Brian's voice roared from the upstairs hall. "You want to burn down the house?"

Prickles of terror shot up her spine. "Brian?" she called.

"Well, turn it off!" he shouted back.

Quickly she pulled on the tight slacks and set off for the kitchen on the run, the pants still unzipped, her hand clutching at the opening.

With the stove turned off, she leaned back against the sink and drew a long breath. What if he had heard? What if he knew?

She was fastening the button on her slacks when Brian entered the kitchen.

He stopped just inside the threshold and looked her over carefully. He hadn't bothered to shave and the shirt he wore belonged in the wash.

"I was making coffee," she said inanely, unable to think of anything sensible to say.

"So I gather," he said drily. "So hurry it up. I've got a head like a busted balloon."

Jennie sniffed. "I don't wonder," she said. "It's not every night you go for a swim in a punch bowl."

He didn't bother to answer. He anchored one hip on the counter beside the sink and watched her fill the coffee pot.

She felt him watching her and the spoon shook in her hand. She had had a lot of things to say to him. A lot of things that had to be said. She couldn't remember any of them. She touched her palm to her forehead. It felt feverish, burning hot. She knew he must see her shame, even if he hadn't heard.

"It was a real son of a bitch," Brian said.

She realized suddenly that he was thinking about the opening at the gallery and not about her at all. Maybe ....

"It was pretty awful," Jennie agreed, glad to keep the conversation on safe territory. "But don't worry too much. After all, Mrs. Whitman did drive us home. And she repeated the invitation for this weekend."

She heard the click of his lighter as he lit a cigarette. Whisps of smoke curled past her and idled out the open door.

"So what?" Brian said. "That bastard husband of hers rides the purse strings in that family. And God, is he tight. The best she can do for me is persuade him to show me at the family gallery."

She set the pot onto a burner and lit a match. "That's something, at least. Do you think he will?"

Brian tugged thoughtfully at an ear lobe. "I wish I knew," he said. "That's what this weekend deal is all about." He gestured disgustedly. "She couldn't even talk him into coming last night. So I have to take the mountain to him."

Jennie frowned. "You mean, he's never even looked at your stuff?"

"Just one," Brian said. "That nude I did of you, right after we were married. The good one. Leigh bought it."

"But ..." Jennie started to protest.

"I know, I know," Brian said quickly. He inhaled deeply and blew a plume of smoke toward the ceiling. "But sometimes a man can't afford to be sentimental, Jen. She wanted the painting. You were running around in a two year old dress and...." He shrugged. "Every man has his price, as they say."

She sat down heavily on the wrought-iron chair. "I'm not sure I appreciate my bare behind hanging in Mrs. Whitman's home."

Brian looked at her squarely. "Why not?" he said. "You don't seem to mind showing it anyplace else."

The scorn, the revulsion in his tone knotted her stomach into a ball. "What are you talking about?" she said. It didn't sound innocent even to her.

"You know damned well what I'm talking about," he said. "I'm talking about Jake and God knows how many others."

She pressed back against the chair, wanting to get away from the accusation in his words, the guilt in her own soul.

"You know," he said, "it's a shame you give it away for free. You could get a good price on the open market and we sure as hell could use the money."

"Brian!"

"Brian!" he mimicked her shocked tone. "Don't you Brian me, kiddo. I had your number a long time ago."

Jennie stood up and gripped the edge of the table with her hands behind her back. "Now I *don't* know what you're talking about," she said.

He leaned away from the cupboard and stood facing her closely. "Oh, don't you," he said. His smile was sickly. "Wouldn't it be nice if you were as sweet and innocent as you look?"

She grabbed his fingers as he reached to touch her. "Stop it," she said. "I don't know what you're talking about."

"Did you really think all this time that I didn't know why you kicked me out of your bedroom?" He took a step toward her. "Did you think I didn't know about you and Jake? All the Jakes?"

She was afraid of him now, even though, for a change, he was sober. She watched his eyes as he spoke.

"You have the guts to tell me you're leaving," he said. "When I should have kicked you into the gutter years ago? You're out having a ball for yourself and I'm supposed to paint? How the hell could any man live with it?"

Jennie bit her lip to hold back the words. There was no sense in trying to outtalk him now. He wouldn't even hear anything she said.

He turned and dropped the butt of his cigarette into the sink. She watched the slowness of his movements, the weighty unhappiness of the man. She wanted to hate him, for all the things he had said, for the lies … and for the truths. But she didn't hate him. She couldn't.

She wanted to fling herself at him. Shout at him that she loved him. That she always had. She wanted him to hear it and believe it.

He turned back to face her and she knew that it was no use. He wouldn't believe her now. Wouldn't believe anything.

"How long did it take you, Jen?" he rasped. His voice sounded like too many cigarettes, too many beers. Maybe he was even crying inside. "How long was it after you married me that you started in with Jake?"

Very quietly, yet with all the firmness she could muster, Jennie said, "Yesterday. I swear to you, Brian, just yesterday. After I decided to leave you."

A flicker of hesitation lighted his eyes. Then he grinned. "And I suppose Jake seduced you?" he said.

Jennie glanced away. Too quickly. "Something like that," she said.

Brian grabbed hold of her shoulders and pulled her forward so hard that her head snapped back on her neck.

"I could kill you for that," he said harshly.

"What—"

"It's bad enough I have to have a wife that's a whore. I don't need you to tell me lies about my best friend."

"But, Brian—"

"You know damned well Jake would never do that to me, Jen." His right hand tightened on her arm. "We've been friends since we were kids."

"He did, Brian. He did," she said desperately.

Brian let go of her with one hand.

She saw it coming, but she couldn't move. His hand caught her on the side of the face and spun her halfway around.

Gasping, sobbing, she gulped for air. Her head felt as though it had been smashed by a truck.

Brian shoved her away from him. "I should have done that years ago," he said. "You're no fit wife for any man."

She felt her knees buckling under her. "Brian ..." she pleaded.

"For chrissake, shut up, will you?" he spat at her. For a moment he stood there, glaring at her as though he wanted to finish her off for good. Then he spun on his heel and stalked out through the living room.

She didn't want him to leave her. Didn't want him to go, hating her like this, believing the things he believed.

"Brian!" she called after him. Her feet moved with a life of their own. She was running, running, skidding along the smooth waxed floor.

The front door slammed.

Jennie stopped in midstride. She couldn't very well go screaming through the streets after him.

He'll be back, she told herself. He'll be back.

And if he didn't come back ....

She threw herself face-down on the sofa, her body shaking with sobs.

CHAPTER FIVE

Jennie watched the first gray light of dawn touch the rooftops of the New York skyline. The yellow café curtains stirred fitfully, damply limp after the night's rain. The rain had helped a little. The air smelled fresher now, cleaner. One could breathe a little oxygen along with the soot. But the forecast said hot. And even the first rays of morning seemed to sizzle the earth's dampness into steam.

She was almost looking forward to the weekend at Oyster Bay. Sand and sea and water. A welcome relief after the long months in the city. She had never complained to Brian about not having the money to get away. She had promised herself in the beginning not to taunt him about keeping up with anybody. She had known when she married him that they might never be rich. But then, she never had been.

Sitting now in her own kitchen, surrounded by things that she had chosen with Brian, Jennie thought of her mother. She hadn't allowed herself to do that for a long time. The woman had been dead for nearly ten years now and still it didn't seem quite real.

It hadn't been until many years after her mother's death that Jennie understood the sacrifices the woman had made to raise her daughter. Spoiled, wilful, vain, Jennie had made demands on her that kept her working far into the night. Stitching, sewing, making party gowns for others so that her own child might have a few of the good things of life. Denying herself everything for the sake of her child, even the medical care and attention that might have saved her.

Jennie had found her there early one morning, sitting in her chair, still holding her needle and a blouse that she had been working on. She had been fourteen then. And broke. Momma's church had buried her. And Momma's daughter had gone out to find a place for herself in the world.

Jennie traced a finger along the pattern of swirls on the table top. She couldn't really blame Brian for the accusations he had hurled at her. He knew, after all, the story of those five years before she met him. But what's a girl supposed to do when she's fourteen and untrained for anything? Too well-developed for the men to let her alone ... and too hungry to care? There had been no one to help her. No one. Her father hadn't been heard from since a week after she was born.

She had made out well with men. Very well. But never had she let herself be just another lay for anybody. She wasn't a whore, no matter what Brian had said. She had gone to school and become a beautician. And she had worked hard, earning good money and saving it. Earning herself the right to decency and a normal life. And the day had come when she was no longer forced to give herself for money, but only for love.

Love for Jennie had always meant Brian.

It had been right for them from the start. For both of them. They had met over beer on a warm summer afternoon and two weeks later they were married. And for the first three years, life had been like a perfect honeymoon.

Jennie sighed and stood up and went to the sink. She turned on the tap and patted droplets of cold water along her cheeks.

How could anything that had started out so simply become such a complicated mess?

Oh, she had realized a long time ago that the thought of her early experiences sickened Brian. She understood that. A man likes to be first with a woman. But he was the best she had ever known. She had tried in every way to let him know it. Yet it must have nagged at him constantly through the years, affecting his work, weakening him as a man, until ....

She glanced at the clock. In a few minutes it would be seven. Nearly sixteen hours since he had stormed out of the house. Where had he gone? She had called Jake, just on a chance. And Smittey, the proprietor at Brian's favorite bar. She had even thought of calling the police. But the realization that he might have gone to another woman had stopped her.

If she never did anything else for Brian, she had to find him in time to keep their appointment with the Whitmans. It probably wouldn't make much of a difference in the long run, but it was his chance, the only one he had left. With a little recognition, a little encouragement about his work, he could still pull himself together, before he reached the stage of alcoholism or suicide. He had become almost lost enough even for that.

At eight, when people were up and moving around, she would start calling. Everyone. All the women Brian had ever known. Jake could tell her who they were. And the hell with her pride. She'd worry about that later.

It wasn't the thought of calling the women in Brian's life that disturbed her so much as the thought of calling Jake again. When she had spoken to him late in the evening, he had been pleasant enough, even humorous. Yet she wasn't at all happy about Jake. If she called too often, he might take it as an encouragement to come back and try again. And that was the one thing she didn't want. Not with Jake or anybody.

She ran water into the sink and dropped in a cake of soap. With a sponge, she rinsed the inside of a cup and set it on the drainboard. She'd drunk enough coffee in the past few hours to float a battleship yet she wasn't hungry. She never could eat and worry all at the same time. And for a change, she couldn't get the worry out of her mind. If she didn't find him soon ....

The front-door chime bonged close beside her— once, and then again. Startled, she let a spoon slip from her fingers to clatter against the sink. It couldn't be Brian. If he'd forgotten his key, he'd be more likely to kick the door in.

Wiping her fingertips hastily on a dishtowel, Jennie set her jaw and lifted her head high, determined to smile no matter who it might be.

Her heels clicked smartly along the bare wooden floor. She got the smile adjusted and swung open the door.

Jake leaned with one shoulder against the doorjamb, his other arm supporting Brian's long, almost limp frame.

"This belong to you?" Jake said.

Jennie sighed. "I'm afraid so," she said. "Where did you find it?"

"Well," Jake said, "I got a little worried after you called. I spent half the damned night lookin' for the bastard. Then when I got back to the apartment, he was asleep in the hall, propped up against my door."

She helped Jake drag him through the doorway and pushed the door shut with her heel. Together, they maneuvered Brian into the living room and onto the couch.

Jake stood looking down at Brian's prostrate figure. "You know, this is getting to be a habit I could live without."

Jennie followed the line of his vision. "That makes two of us," she said.

"Maybe the kid needs a doctor," Jake said, not looking at her.

Jennie realized that Jake was deliberately avoiding meeting her glance. A flush of shame warmed her cheeks. "I don't think he's ill," she said gently. "Just unhappy, Jake."

Jake nodded. "That's what I mean," he said. "There are doctors for that, too."

Jennie's eyes widened in surprise. "You mean a psychiatrist?"

"Yeah. Like me and all the other guys who're unhappy."

Jennie smiled down fondly at her husband. "I wouldn't suggest it, if I were you. Brian's strictly from the self-help school."

"Yeah," Jake said. "So I see." He turned and started to edge his way toward the door. "But keep it in mind, Jen. I know a real good man, if he's interested."

"Jake, look at me," Jennie said quietly.

He hesitated, but did not glance up.

She put her hand on his arm. "Look at me, Jake," she repeated.

He couldn't manage to face her directly, but she realized that he had tried.

"You know as well as I do what's the matter with Brian," she said evenly. "He knows about us, Jake. And he thinks I'm reverting to past behavior. You know what I was before he married me."

She saw the shadow of fear flicker across his eyes.

"How does he know about us?"

"I guess he heard," she said. "Or saw. I don't know." She gestured impatiently. "What difference does it make how? He knows, that's all."

Jake pulled away from the touch of her hand on his arm. "Jesus," he breathed. He glanced at Brian. "He could kill me without half trying."

With all she had recently learned about Jake, his words surprised her. He didn't give a damn about Brian. Or about her. As long as he saved his own neck....

"You don't have to worry," she said. "He won't."

"What?"

"I said, he won't. He blames me for everything. After all, a man's best friend is sacred. Isn't he, Jake?"

Jake took another step toward the door. "So I'm as big a bastard as he is," he said.

"You're worse than he'll ever be." Her voice held the faint edge of hysteria. She could have smashed his fat, greedy face.

Jake stood very still, his amber eyes dark with anger. "Take it easy," he said quietly. "You're not all that goddamned innocent." He gestured toward her. "For chrissake, look at yourself. You wear your clothes so damned tight, I don't even have to take 'em off to know what it looks like. What do you expect from a guy, when you shove it in his face like that?"

The truth of his words slashed at her like a whip. She looked down at the front of her dress, tight all the way down as a second skin. She felt him watching her. Prickles of apprehension jabbed along her spine.

"Yeah," he said. "Ripe and juicy and free for the taking."

His arm shot out and his strong fingers grabbed at her breast.

She lashed out at him with both hands, striking for his face. She heard him laugh. Then one hand closed over her wrists and he slammed her back against the wall.

His face moved in close to hers. "You could drive a man crazy," he said hoarsely.

He flattened the length of his torso against her.

Her head cracked against the wall. Sparks of pain danced behind her eyelids. "Let me go," she breathed. "Let me go."

His hand moved in between them. "I owe you something," he said. "I shouldn't've left you hung up like that."

Beyond his shoulder, she saw Brian stir on the couch. He turned his head toward them.

"Let me go," she said again, almost screaming now, wanting Brian to hear, to help her.

Brian's mouth sagged open. He began to snore.

Jake's fingers tore at the skirt of her dress. She felt him yanking it up, caressing her naked thigh. Touching her greedily. She hadn't bothered with panties. They wouldn't have stopped him for a minute. She sagged against him.

The sound of Brian's snoring filled her ears, pounded inside her head. She shut her eyes to close out the sight of him. She wanted to die. Right here. Right now.

Jake heaved against her relentlessly, savagely.

She felt like he was trying to rip the guts out of her. Her body screamed with pain. She heard her buttocks slapping against the wall. But there was no ecstasy, no burst of sensation. Only the pain.

He had held her against the wall with his body. Now, as he moved away from her, she felt her knees buckling under her.

He didn't try to stop her fall. She went down on her knees. And then she was sitting on the floor, her legs curled under her.

"Remember me for this one," Jake said.

She heard him turn and walk briskly toward the door. It slammed shut behind him.

For a long time she sat there, hunched over miserably, hugging her legs against her. She had gotten what she deserved, finally. What she deserved for all the years of using men. What she deserved for the way she had treated Brian. She couldn't even feel sorry for herself. The ugly bruises on the insides of her thighs, the hot pain shooting up her back. She deserved all of it and more.

Slowly, she pulled herself up, using the wall for support. Brian still snored unconsciously on the couch. He would never know what Jake had done to them. Probably wouldn't believe it if he had seen it for himself. It was better that way. Let him cling to Jake, if he wanted to. He needed someone. And God knew, Jake probably wasn't much worse than she herself had been all these years.

In the downstairs lavatory, Jennie ran cool water into the sink and cupped her hands. She buried her face in the soothing liquid. The jangle of her nerves throbbed through her. With a shaky hand, she outlined a soft mouth and touched a powder puff to her cheekbones.

Both she and Brian would need a lot of repairs before they were ready to face the Whitmans. Remembering the business before them, Jennie felt a sudden charge of energy and set hastily to work.

The job of sobering up Brian was something that had become almost second nature by now. Sobering him up for an appointment, sobering him up to feed him, sobering him up to shove him in front of the easel to paint. She poured a tall glass full of tomato juice and opened a fresh vacuum can of coffee. Maybe she ought to let him sleep for a while, at least get the rage out of his system. But she didn't want him to face Dirk Whitman looking like a drunken bum.

Kneeling beside the couch, she forced him to raise his head enough to swallow the tomato juice. Dribbles of it ran down his chin and she wiped them off with the napkin she had remembered she would need.

He gulped noisily and gagged. His hand struck out clumsily, shoving away the glass.

"You're going to drink it," she muttered, "if I have to pour it up your nose." She held the glass firmly to his lips.

Finally the glass was empty. He hadn't opened his eyes, but she knew the juice would work like a magic potion. It always did.

Brian hoisted himself to a sitting position. Still with his eyes closed, he shoved himself away from the couch and lurched toward the door of the lavatory.

She stepped forward to help. He brushed her aside and went into the tiny room.

She heard the sound of him retching, heaving as though he wanted to turn himself inside out. She leaned a shoulder against the wall and pressed her palm to her forehead. It killed her to see him like this, to watch him killing himself. And yet there was no way for her to help him. Maybe no way for anyone.

He was finished finally. She heard him gasping convulsively for air. She went into the room and stood beside him.

"Can I help?" she said.

"Le' me alone." He reached for the tap and sent cold water splashing into the bowl.

Jennie held out a wash cloth. "Here," she said. "Put this on your head."

He struck out at her savagely. "Le' me alone."

From long experience, she ducked the blow easily and stepped back out of his reach. "There's coffee in the kitchen," she said. "Let me know when you're ready."

She left him then, moving briskly through the living room and out to the kitchen. She poured water from the kettle into the coffeepot and set it aside to drip through. Idly she realized that neither of them had eaten for two days. She wasn't hungry now. With enough arguing, they could keep the food bills down to nothing. Except for the coffee.

She set out mugs for both of them. In a minute he would come in, throw himself down on a chair, drink three mugs of coffee and apologize. He hadn't gotten beyond that stage yet. He still apologized for everything. It was like he had never in his life done something for the sheer hell of it. But always because he had to. Because he couldn't help himself. Like he was driven, by fear or maybe the demon of his genius. But forever driven.

She filled the mugs and sat down at the far side of the table, facing the door, waiting for him to appear. She had no idea if he would remember the scene between them yesterday. She never knew what he might remember. Or forget. Sometimes he lost a whole day. And then he would be frightened a little and for maybe a week he would remain sober. Then he would forget the fear, too. And the drinking began again.

She heard him bump heavily against a chair and stiffened, wary of facing him. Afraid for herself, but more afraid for him.

He did not sit down at the table. Instead, he took the cup and carried it to the sink. She watched him take a swallow, then set the cup down.

She waited for him to say something. Even hello. Or drop dead or anything. But he stared at the tip of one shoe and seemed to have forgotten that she was there.

She could stand almost anything better than the silent treatment. The God-awful torment of being ignored. In a good fight, she could fare as well as anyone. But like this, she sort of shriveled up inside and died.

Finally she could stand it no longer. "Well?" she said.

He looked up at her as though he had never seen her before and didn't much like what he saw now. "Well what?"

A pulse began to throb sickeningly in her throat. She had never known him like this before. And she didn't know how to handle him. The wrong word now....

"Jake brought you home," she said.

He grunted.

"He found you in the hall outside his door. Passed out."

He shrugged. "So?"

Her eyebrows arched in surprise. No shame, no apology? "Jake thinks you should see an analyst," she said evenly. "You're going to kill yourself if you keep drinking like this."

"Do I give a damn what Jake thinks?" he said savagely. "Or you? Or anybody else?" He poked his chest with a forefinger. "Me. That's what I care about. Do you hear? *Me.*"

It was a new line for Brian. But if he meant it, it was the best thing she had ever heard. He still had a lot of life ahead of him. And maybe, if she was lucky, maybe after he got himself straightened out, there would still be a chance for them. Maybe he would want her then, as she still wanted him.

"Brian," she said tentatively, "maybe if we got away from the city for a while, we could see things more clearly. You know, get a new perspective on life and work out all the things that have gone wrong between us."

He took another swallow of coffee and kept his glance averted from hers. "I thought you were leaving me," he said.

That much he hadn't forgotten. And if he remembered that, he must also remember....

"I didn't mean that, Brian," she said gently. "I was upset and hurt...."

"And you thought we could kiss and make up?"

She opened her lips to speak, but he cut her short with a wave of his hand.

"It's not that simple, Jennifer," he said. "*I* want a divorce now. On the grounds of adultery."

He grinned and her heart sank.

"Like I said, all I care about now is me." He paused to let the point sink in. "And I've already been to the lawyer."

CHAPTER SIX

From her seat several rows behind him, Jennie stared at the top of her husband's head. It had been a relief to find the train crowded with families getting an early start on the weekend. He hadn't spoken a word to her since early morning, except to tell her to hurry the packing. And she certainly had nothing worth saying to him.

He had phoned Leigh just before they left to arrange for someone to meet the train. Ordinarily they would have borrowed Jake's car. But today, neither of them had mentioned it. For her part, Jennie would have been happy never to see Jake again. But she had no intention of letting Brian have an uncontested divorce on his grounds. And she would need Jake as a witness.

It seemed almost impossible to Jennie that her future should depend on someone she had come to despise as much as she had Jake. His selfishness, his greed revolted her to the core of her being. At her worst, she had never been as low as Jake was low. She had never tried to deceive anyone about her intentions. And what little she got, she paid for in full.

Yet she had come to understand Jake well enough to realize that this time she would have to be deceptive, even dishonest in order to get what she wanted from him. If she could only make him believe that she had been overpowered and won by his display of masculine virility.... With an ego like Jake's, it shouldn't be too difficult at all.

She leaned an elbow on the window ledge and turned her attention to the scenery flitting past the window. Behind her a child that had been fussy since they left the city began to cry. Passengers, nerves already frayed by the stifling heat of the stuffy car, the reek of cigarette smoke and dust and bodies, shifted restlessly and grumbled among themselves. She hardly noticed the noise or the discomfort of the car. She was seeing trees, for a change. And flowers and grass. Even a cow. She had hoped that one day she and Brian might be able to afford a place on the Island. A quiet, safe place, away from the city's noise and filth. A place to raise children and grow old together.

She glanced at him then, wondering if he still remembered the plans, the dreams they had once shared.

His head tilted back against the seat and he appeared to be sleeping. He had sobered up completely, she knew, but even now he looked like he was sleeping off a hangover—something about the way his head hung to the side, drooping, bobbing with the motion of the train. He looked spineless somehow, limp like a rag doll thrown down on the seat.

She could hate him all she wanted to now. He had made it clear that he hated her. Yet, looking at him, she felt the rise of all the old ambivalent feelings she had always felt toward him. Feelings she had never been able to straighten out in her head. Feelings that made her want him when she hated him, reject him when she loved him. She knew that it would never change for her. Not really. Now that he had rejected her, she wanted him more than she ever had before.

But thinking was useless. She needed to do something. Something active and positive. And maybe this weekend, away from the pressures of the city.... At least, they'd be sharing a bedroom. He was far too virile a man to ignore her in bed.

A smile touched her lips as she outlined in her mind a plan of seduction. She had known Brian a long time and very well. She knew what he liked ... and she was more than ready to give it to him.

Absorbed with her thoughts, Jennie hardly noticed the miles flying past outside the window, the touch of freshness in the air as the train moved along the edge of the Sound. She didn't even hear the conductor call out the stop at Oyster Bay.

She felt a touch on her shoulder and started. Looking up, she saw Brian waiting on line with the suitcase in his hand. He stared straight ahead, his jaw set in a determined line.

He's nervous, she thought. Scared.

She got up and smoothed down the front of her skirt. Deliberately, she had worn the least seductive garment she owned. With Jake's accusation still ringing in her ears, she had spent several hours unlearning all the chic she had ever known. She had seen the question in Brian's eyes. And something almost like appreciation. But it wasn't Brian who interested her now.

The train ground to a halt and the long line inched forward. She watched him leap from the bottom step to the concrete platform and start away from the train without waiting for her.

She followed his long-legged stride, almost running to keep up with him.

His free hand went up in a wave and she heard him shout hello. His stride stretched into a run.

At the end of a line of parked cars, Leigh Whitman waited for them in her big, black Lincoln. She had lowered the convertible top and sat on the back of the front seat, her knees up, feet propped against the wheel.

A hell of a position for a forty-year-old woman, was Jennie's first thought.

But on her it looks good, was her second.

Realizing that even on the comfortable heels she was wearing she couldn't keep up with Brian, Jennie slowed her pace to an easy walk and took her time about reaching the car. Brian swung the suitcase into the rear seat and began an animated conversation with Leigh. He was talking with both hands as though his mouth wouldn't go fast enough to get it all out. Not once did he look around for his wife.

At Jennie's approach, Leigh broke off in the middle of a sentence and turned to smile at her. "Here you are," she said. She turned to Brian. "Shall we go?"

Without waiting for an answer, she slid down from the back of the seat and moved over to let him take the wheel. She leaned over to open the door on Jennie's side of the car.

Jennie didn't at all like the idea of the woman being between herself and Brian. Even in the tight fitting slacks and a man-tailored white shirt, Leigh was more attractive than any woman Jennie had even seen. Even the bare feet looked good.

She slid in beside the woman while Brian got in behind the wheel. She reached out for the door handle.

Leigh leaned across her suddenly. Her bare arm touched Jennie's breasts and, for a fraction of an instant, lingered there.

Jennie pressed herself tight against the back of the seat, thinking to get out of the woman's way. Yet she felt the arm move with her, brushing against her ever so slightly as the woman slammed the door.

Leigh settled back into her seat and resumed the conversation with Brian.

For a few moments, as Brian swung the car in a wide curve and out onto the highway, Jennie listened to their words, trying to find in herself an enthusiasm about who was showing what at which gallery. She had never really cared. That was the business end of art and the part that bored her. But the two of them apparently knew every artist and every gallery in town. And cared very much. Jennie realized to her dismay that the common interest Leigh shared with her husband gave the woman a definite edge. If she wanted it.

She settled back in the glare of sunlight and let her thoughts drift idly. Yet not without aim. She found herself considering the woman beside her, remembering the touch that might have been an accident, but almost certainly wasn't. She turned her head slightly and studied Leigh's profile. What was happening inside that beautiful head?

There was certainly nothing about the woman's appearance to indicate any peculiar motives for her behavior. And surely her interest in Brian seemed genuine enough. Yet Jennie had lived in the Village long enough to have seen and learned many things. And the one thing she understood best was that you couldn't tell anything about a person's sex life until you had climbed into bed with him. Oh, sure, Leigh was wearing slacks and she had short hair. But Jennie herself wore slacks, and short hair in the summertime was no novelty anywhere. Still, there was something intangible there that stirred Jennie's curiosity and, in a way, intrigued her. Not for any interest that Leigh Whitman might have in her. She couldn't care less about Leigh. Couldn't care less about any woman that way. But because of Brian's infatuation.

She smiled to herself, in a perverse way almost enjoying the thought of Brian's being lured into making a fool of himself over the woman. It would serve him right. For she believed now his insistence that he had never slept with Leigh, and she could even believe that he never would— Not if Leigh were really that way. Not if she really dug women, the way it seemed. Yet, if it were true, where did Dirk Whitman fit into the picture?

Jennie was suddenly very glad that they had made this trek out to the Island. It ought to prove a lot more interesting than a weekend of fighting back home.

They turned off the main road and onto a graveled drive. Low-hanging branches skimmed above their heads as the car sped along. From somewhere off to the left, she heard a whistle hoot as a boat came in for a landing. She couldn't see the water yet or hear it, but the smell of it was everywhere, clean and salty, invigorating.

"We're on Centre Island now," Leigh said, directing her words to Jennie. "You'll see the house in a few minutes. I still get a kick every time I see it."

She followed the line of Leigh's vision toward what looked like a clump of trees on a hilltop. The car crunched around a sharp bend in the road and began climbing slowly up a steep incline. The road here looked as though it had been hacked out of the heart of the forest, with trees growing close together all around them, their roots stretching now and then onto the road-bed itself. High above, the branches from both sides bent over the road to meet in a leafy canopy almost shutting out the sun.

Jennie got the creepy feeling of being underground in a secret passageway, like in the stories she used to make up when she was a kid. In a minute she would be in the ogre's castle, far underground, in the torture room where he kept little girls tied to racks and beat them.

Lost for a moment in the nightmare world of her childhood fantasies, Jennie shivered, feeling frightened suddenly, yet afraid to cry out for fear the ogre might hear. She put one hand on either side of her on the leather seat, bracing herself for whatever lay ahead.

Leigh's warm palm closed over her hand, soothingly, as though she too had known the childhood dreams and were reliving them now with Jennie.

At her touch, Jennie came back with a shock to the present. Feeling a little foolish for her momentary lapse into the past, she turned to smile reassuringly at Leigh. She found the woman peering at her intently.

"I'm all right," Jennie said. She wanted her to stop staring like that, holding her hand as if she were feeble-minded and unable to fend for herself.

Still Leigh's hand pressed warmly against her own.

Suddenly the car shot out of the mouth of the tree tunnel and they were bumping across a rocky shelf of ground. Just as suddenly, Leigh withdrew her hand from Jennie's and pointed straight ahead. "There," she breathed.

Jennie followed the pointing finger to the ugliest pile of stone that anyone had ever called home. Indeed, it was a castle, every hideous inch and soaring turret of it. Here and there a tiny window poked through the masses of clinging ivy and Jennie found herself counting, wondering how long it would take to dust all those rooms.

"It's authentic," Leigh informed her. "Dirk's grandfather had it brought over stone by stone from Scotland. Nobody's ever been able to figure out why." She smiled. "The natives around here call it the Dungeon."

Jennie could well understand the local reaction. "How can you live in it?" she asked impulsively. "I mean ...."

Leigh laughed easily. "I know exactly what you mean," she said. "When Dirk and I first moved out here from the city——" She broke off to glance at Jennie, "—he got everything when his father died, including the monstrosity—when we first moved in, it smelled like an outhouse. We've had the whole thing redone inside. It's quite livable now. Isn't it, Brian?"

Jennie glanced past the woman's head to study her husband's face.

He grunted, but kept his attention on the road.

So he's not even bothering to be civil, Jennie thought, a little surprised that he had brought their mutual hostility out into the open. It wasn't like Brian to let the neighbors in on the sordid details of his private life. But maybe ....

What if he knew about Leigh? What if he had seen Leigh's furtive handclasp in the dark tunnel of trees? If he had intended to make out with Leigh this weekend, to woo her into sponsoring a showing at the Whitman gallery, he surely wouldn't welcome competition from his own wife.

Not that she intended to give him any. Once out of the tight confines of the car, she would make sure to avoid Leigh as best she could. But Brian wouldn't realize that. He probably thought she'd let Leigh make a play for her just for spite. But Jennie wasn't having any of that. If there were going to be any acrobatics this weekend ....

Brian slammed the car to a halt before a gargoyled entrance-way. He got out on his side of the car and reached toward the back seat.

Leigh slid across the front seat and got out beside him. She put her hand on his arm. "Leave it," she said. "Arthur will pick it up."

Jennie waited for Brian to come around to open her door, as he had always done. When he made no motion to do so, she opened the door herself and stepped out onto the drive.

Leigh turned to look for her. "Come on," she said. "We have to check in with the lord of the manor before his curiosity kills him."

Jennie watched Leigh and Brian set off briskly on a pathway leading around the side of the house. She felt foolish standing there, even more foolish tagging after them like an unwanted kid sister. She sighed, seeing no choice for herself but to follow them. If Brian wanted to act like a spoiled child, there wasn't much she could do about it. And if Leigh's interest were confined to hold-ing hands in dark corners, there wasn't much she could do about that either.

Pulling her stomach in tight and thrusting her chin high, Jennie trailed after them to the back of the house and onto a flag-stone terrace extending the length of the monstrous old house and some fifty feet in width, ending abruptly at a stone wall bor-dering the edge of a sheer drop down to the water.

If Dirk Whitman's curiosity were killing him, he might already be dead, from the looks of him. He lay sprawled on his stomach on a rubber mattress spread out on the paving. He looked huge and hairless, his tanned, hard-muscled body smooth and glistening with perspiration. Completely bald, his head was as deeply tanned and perspiring as the rest of him.

Leigh walked over to the mattress and jabbed her bare toes into her husband's ribs. "Put on your manners," she said. "We've got company."

He jumped up instantly, like a trained athlete coming out of a push up position. He gave a tug at the belt of his bikini briefs.

Jennie had the feeling that even the inadequate loin cloth was a concession to his guests. There was something almost obscene about the man's obvious enjoyment of his own physique. Something about the way he moved repelled her with its obvious narcissism. Still, she had to admit that she had never seen anything quite like Dirk Whitman. Certainly rarely seen quite so much of anyone. The man was immense.

He took her hand and gazed intently into her eyes. "Mrs. Dunbar," he said, his voice mellow and rich, as though aged for centuries in the barrel of his chest.

He frightened her just a little, with the hugeness of himself, the complete hairlessness even to the absence of eyebrows, and the strange, almost maniacal intensity of his black eyes. Yet, the way he shook her hand, the way he smiled like a self-conscious child reassured any misgivings she might have had. She understood now why Leigh Whitman thought of men as little boys with long tails, for there was something truly childlike about this man she had married. It was somehow as though he were a grotesque, oversized infant, naked almost as the day he was born and emotionally as defenseless.

She watched him cross to welcome Brian, hunching his shoulders a little as though embarrassed to tower over another man. Brian shook hands with him briefly. She saw the look of disgust and loathing in Brian's eyes and wondered if it were as apparent to the Whitmans as it was to her.

If Dirk sensed Brian's feelings, he gave no indication. He asked a few questions about Brian's recent opening, tactfully, obviously having heard the whole story from Leigh. Then he took Brian's elbow and steered him away to the edge of the terrace. Their voices lowered, keeping their conversation an intimate thing between them.

"Come on over here," Leigh said, "and we'll make ourselves comfortable." She gestured toward the men. "They seem to have forgotten we're here."

Jennie laughed suddenly, startled by the note of tolerance in Leigh's tone. For herself, she was deathly curious to know what Dirk Whitman had to say to Brian that seemed so dreadfully serious.

"Don't worry," Leigh said, sensing her thoughts. She sprawled out on a lounge chair and patted the seat of the one beside her.

Jennie sat down cautiously on the edge of the seat, wanting to appear as comfortable as possible, yet keeping her distance from Leigh.

"They're talking business," Leigh went on. She wiggled her toes in the warm sunlight. "Dirk's agreed to let Brian have a special exhibit at the gallery."

"What?" Jennie blurted. The way the woman said it, anyone might have thought it was something that happened for Brian every day.

Leigh took a cigarette from the pack lying beside her on the table and offered one to Jennie. When Jennie shook her head, she lit her own and leaned back against the chair. "I'm a little annoyed with him about the whole thing," she said.

"Oh?" Jennie breathed, feeling the tendrils of red tape spinning out to choke off Brian's future.

"Hmm," Leigh answered. "The gallery is Dirk's special baby, you know." She waited for Jennie's nod. "And he's a damned snob about what he'll hang. I don't really have any say in the matter at all." She shrugged. "Anyhow, Dirk likes a certain kind of ultra-modern stuff that I can't stomach. You know, these things that look like crap smeared on a john wall."

Jennie smiled stiffly, anxious for Leigh to get down to the point. She didn't give a damn about Dirk Whitman's taste in art. But if Brian could get a showing at the Whitman gallery, she could forget about him, at least as far as his career was concerned. And with that problem taken care of, they could do something about the rest. Something.

"So he's being difficult," Leigh went on.

"In what way?" Jennie asked, trying to sound patient, but hearing the annoyance in her tone.

Leigh's right eyebrow arched slightly. "Who can ever tell with Dirk?" she said simply.

Jennie looked up as a bony old man in baggy dungarees came out onto the terrace, carrying a tray of drinks. He moved slowly, as though his energy had gone into retirement years ago. Shaggy-faced, his fingers swollen at the knuckles and stiff, he shuffled across to them and set the tray heavily onto a glass-topped table. Without glancing at either of them, he withdrew toward the door from which he had left the house.

"That," Leigh said, "is Arthur. He's one of the prize relics in this museum."

"You inherited him, too?" Jennie said, amused by the dour old man.

"Of course," Leigh said. "We wouldn't have a roof over our heads if it were up to Dirk to earn it."

She sensed the warm affection the woman had for her husband and found herself more curious than ever about the strange pair. Before she could consider them further, Dirk's voice cut into her thoughts.

"It's settled," he said to no one in particular. He turned back to Brian. "We'll drink to it?"

"We'll drink to it," Brian echoed. He took the glass Dirk held out to him and raised it instantly to his lips.

She watched him take a long swallow, lower the glass, then drink again. Whatever he had just agreed to, he wasn't feeling good about it. A tremor of nervousness, almost of foreboding, chilled through her.

"What's settled?" Leigh asked.

"About the gallery," Brian said. "Two months from today."

Jennie started to tell him how pleased she felt. But something about the way he said it warned her to keep still.

Leigh looked up at her husband. "No strings?" she said.

"One or two," Dirk answered. He moved to stand beside his wife, his huge hand on the back of her neck. "Little strings. Without nooses."

Jennie glanced quickly at Brian and found him watching her.

He turned away at her glance and for a moment lowered his head. Then, smiling at some private thought, he raised the glass and drank.

CHAPTER SEVEN

Jennie turned off the babble of their voices and relaxed against the cool, worn leather of the sofa. Through half-lowered eyelids, she gazed across the wide room at the portrait of herself. The naked, languid, sleepy-eyed pose that Brian had painted shortly after their marriage. She had thought it a marvelous painting when he had just finished it. Thought it the most sensual thing she had ever seen. Yet looking at it now, she realized that it wasn't really very good at all, neither as a painting nor as a picture of her. What she had once seen as sensuality now appeared as a sick sort of lust, almost a kind of perversion. He had captured none of the essence of her, none of the good in her that loved him and wanted to be his wife. Only the ugliness, the greed and the wanton uselessness that had characterized her before he came into her life.

Perhaps, she realized, he had never really seen the other side of her, the side that could have been faithful to him, could have cherished their relationship. Perhaps he had never really understood or accepted her as she really was. For Jennie knew, as Brian had never known, that the girl in the painting —the lusty, sex-starved creature he had portrayed —was not truly Jennie at all.

Yet there she was— A Girl Called Jennie—hung in the library of the Whitmans' home for all the world to see. And she resented somehow this thing he had done to her, this lie he had told about her in oil and lacquer. Resented having Dirk and Leigh come to know, and apparently like very well, something about her that she could not accept about herself.

She closed her eyes and let herself drift into a state of almost sleep. She felt that she had probably never been quite so tired—nor so bored—in her life. The conversation and the alcohol had dribbled on through the night and she had found no solace in either. Brian had openly ignored her all evening and Dirk and Leigh, apparently taking their cue from him, had done the same, except to fill her full of food she wasn't hungry for and drinks that had made her head throb.

When at last they had come in from the terrace, theoretically to retire, she had found herself rejoicing in the final hope of being able to stretch out and sleep. But the others obviously still weren't ready to call it a night. The bottles and the ice came out once more.

Jennie at least knew when to stop. One more drink and she would pass out on the floor. Instead, she had thrown herself down on the sofa, determined to grab at least a few minutes' nap, but the sight of that damned portrait, the image of it imprinted on her brain even after she had closed her eyes, would not let her rest. Here was Brian's opinion of her, smeared across canvas for any eyes to devour and the quality of it embarrassed and humiliated her. She turned her back to the wall on which it hung and buried her face against the smooth leather.

She had barely settled herself when she sensed a change in the tenor of the conversation behind her. She heard Leigh's voice raise excitedly and Brian seconding whatever it was she had said.

In a moment, Brian's hand touched her shoulder. Shook her demandingly. "Get up," he said, his voice fuzzy with drink, his words thick. "We're going for a swim."

For a moment Jennie thought she must have misunderstood. Yet behind Brian, her hand resting on his waist, Leigh stood waiting anxiously for Jennie to stir herself.

"What? What?" Jennie heard the confusion in her voice and realized that she was at least half asleep.

"Come on," Leigh insisted. "A swim before breakfast …." She gestured expansively.

Stiffly, Jennie sat up and tugged the skirt over her knees. Her head felt like an alcoholic's nightmare. "I usually have breakfast after a night's sleep," she grumbled.

She felt Brian waiting impatiently. She glanced up at him. "Brian, are you sure you're in any condition … ?"

"Come on, get the lead out," he said roughly.

She knew it would do her no good to argue. She couldn't out-talk all three of them. Even Dirk, who looked so easygoing, fidgeted nervously in the background.

Sighing, Jennie stood up. Her legs felt heavy, her feet like lumps of lead. A swim in the icy, dawn water of the Sound was the last thing she wanted right now. But she couldn't very well let Brian go off without her, in his condition. Not if she ever expected to collect alimony from the drunken sot. At the moment, she couldn't think of him as anything else.

She followed him out of the living room and down the long hallway to the stairs. He went up slowly, pulling himself along by the bannister. She almost wished he would fall flat on his face. Go to sleep right there where he fell.

Upstairs, she stepped past him and walked ahead of him down the hall and into the apartment where they had already been sent to "freshen up." Arthur had done a neat job of unpacking their bag, arranging everything carefully in the carved mahogany dresser and the wall-length closet. Everything in the room looked as antique as the room itself. Yet she had to admit that it was comfortable. The huge canopied bed with its silk sheets and big puffy pillows looked exquisitely clean and soft as a cloud.

She turned her attention away from the bed and rooted in the top drawer of the dresser for their suits and the terrycloth robes she had remembered to pack. Her city-soft flesh revolted at the thought of the cold, damp beach and of having to stretch out on the wet sand.

She threw the suits disgustedly on the nubby white bed spread. "I could kill you," she thrust at Brian. "Can't you do anything anymore but make a damned fool of yourself?"

In his anger, he ripped a button off his shirt trying to open it. He kept his back to her, yet she saw the dark-red rage creep into his cheeks and up the back of his neck.

She didn't have the strength to fight with him. And she didn't really care. If she just got through this weekend.... She felt as though she were surrounded by a band of maniacs. She needed an aspirin—and coffee. Gallons of coffee.

She picked up his clothes as he dropped them to the floor. Even so, she had undressed and pulled on the tight black suit before he'd peeled down to his shorts. She stood in front of the full length mirror, tugging at the hem of her suit, trying to look adequately covered in a scrap of cloth about the size of a Kleenex. She hadn't wanted to wear it, hadn't wanted to wear anything like it after the accusations Jake had hurled at her. But it was the only one she had.

"Where's the goddamned suit?" Brian said irritably.

She turned away from the sight of his nakedness, ugly and whiskey-bloated to her now. He looked like a bull ape, all of him covered with thick, coarse black hair despite the soft blondeness of his head. She could remember when she had found him attractive, had loved to rub against him and tug at the coarse growth with her lips. Now he merely looked disgusting, almost obscene.

"On the bed," she said patiently. "Where you saw me throw it."

"I didn't see you throw it," he said belligerently. "If I saw you throw it, I'd throw it back at you."

"Oh, Brian, for heaven's sake," she said. "The Whitmans are probably waiting for us. We haven't got time to argue."

"That's right," he said. "That's right. We haven't even got anything to argue about." He stepped clumsily into the trunks and began pulling them up his legs. He wobbled unsteadily, like a fat woman fighting a girdle.

She had almost forgotten that he hadn't been speaking to her. The restless tension between them now had become so much a part of their lives that it seemed somehow natural. Glancing at the puzzled frown on his face, she realized that he had been feeling the same thing. Had forgotten for the moment the newborn hatred between them. Had even forgotten that he was suing her for divorce.

She watched the memory flood back into his consciousness. Watched the slackness go out of his jaw and tighten into determination and loathing. She had lost him again. Whatever little she had still held onto.

He stood up and straightened his shoulders. He took the light-weight robe she held out to him and hung it over his arm. Without glancing at her again, without bothering to speak, he turned on his heel and stalked toward the door.

He wasn't bumbling along now in a drunken stupor. He was walking like a man. An angry, outraged one, but like a man. She felt a surge of something very like respect for him now. It didn't matter that he had dismissed her, had turned his back on her with such finality. All that mattered was that he had reared back on his hind legs and faced up to .... To something. She didn't know what. She didn't care. But something had happened inside his head, something positive.

Loving him, loving him desperately, more afraid now than ever of losing him, Jennie hastily grabbed up her beach robe and hurried after him down the stairs.

The three of them were already on the terrace, waiting for her. Thankfully she saw that the morning sun had already broken through the haze hanging over the shore-line. As she stepped after Dirk onto the winding path that led down to the beach, she looked ahead and down to the water. The Whitmans' private beach stretched in a half moon around a shallow cove. She had been told earlier that Grandfather Whitman had had the cove blasted out of the sheer rock and she looked about her as they moved slowly downward. The path itself was hardly more than a scratch cut on the shale surface, but the old man had been wise enough to provide an iron railing all the way down. She clung to it almost desperately, leaning against it heavily to counterbalance the slippery rubber soles of her beach shoes. The complete bleakness of the scene, the chill of the early-morning air nipped sharply at her nerves, and she felt herself moving now with her eyes closed, afraid to look down, afraid even to look back up the steep incline to the terrace wall.

The others went forward easily, Leigh leading the way, as though they had travelled the path often enough to have forgotten its dangers, or to have mastered them. The thought crossed her mind that Brian, too, had made this trip often before. She felt foolish, remembering how sorry she had often felt for him, confined to the city and the stuffy studio on the third floor of their Village home.

She pushed all thought of Brian away from her and concentrated on the more immediate matter of saving her own neck. When at last she stepped onto level ground, she felt completely enervated, ready to collapse in a heap right where she was.

Brian and Dirk tossed their robes onto the sand and set off on the run down to the water's edge. She watched Brian hurl himself headlong into the shallow waves. Feeling the chill that must have shocked through him, she shivered and pulled the robe tight around her.

Leigh laughed close beside her. "Here," she said amiably. Sit down on this. Wrap it around you, if you want." She held out the red-and-blue checkered blanket that she had carried down the precipice, slung casually over her shoulder.

Jennie could have slapped her, standing there in her bare feet, looking warm, relaxed and as serene as though she had slept all night. She took one end of the blanket and, with Leigh's help, spread it out.

She had expected the sand to be damp and dreary. But the hot sun of many days had baked into it relentlessly, leaving it dry and almost cozily warm. She kicked off her sandals and dug her toes into its warmth at the edge of the blanket.

"That's better," Leigh commented. "It's really quite a lovely place, if you'd just relax enough to enjoy it."

She dropped down on the far side of the blanket and leaned back with her arms hugged around her legs. Her eyes sparkled with amusement.

Jennie turned her glance toward the water, unable to bear the way Leigh looked at her. "Yes," she said tightly, "it is lovely here." Indeed, she supposed it was, if one were part mountain goat and the other half idiot. She had looked forward with a kind of glee to being at the seaside, but now that she was here, she felt like a damned fool. She couldn't shake off the headache that nagged at her. Nor the dreadful thought that eventually she would have to climb back up to the house.

Maybe she wouldn't. Maybe she would just stay here forever. Stay here and sleep for a month. Let them drop food over the side in a basket. Or let them leave her to starve. Either way, it didn't matter. She just wanted to stretch out ....

She started to lie back on the blanket when suddenly she remembered Leigh sitting there, watching her. Probably still smirking in that damned complacent way of hers. She groaned inwardly and leaned her forehead against her knees.

"What's bothering you?" Leigh asked quietly. "You've been looking half dead since dinner time."

Jennie sighed. "I'm just getting old, I guess."

"That's a good one," Leigh commented. "Girl, you're hardly more than half my age. Suppose you had half a dozen kids to chase after. What would you do then?"

Jennie sat very still, shocked into immobility by the woman's words. How could she have hit so squarely upon the source of all

Jennie's unhappiness, her problems with Brian? And what could she say to the woman, how could she find an answer for a question that had none?

"Well?" Leigh prodded.

"I...I don't know," Jennie choked out. She tried to keep her tone light. It was none of Leigh's business, after all. "I suppose I'd have to take vitamins."

"Maybe you ought to try it," Leigh said, but very gently. "A man needs a little companionship, you know. And Brian certainly enjoys...."

She didn't want to hear from another woman what her husband enjoyed. Certainly not from this one. "Damn Brian!" she blurted irritably.

"Oh?" Her voice was throaty with curiosity. And with something else.

Jennie heard the insinuation in Leigh's tone and immediately regretted her words. Yet she had been sincere enough. The woman must have sensed it.

"Yes," she said flatly. "I meant that. I'm sick and tired of hearing what Brian wants and what Brian needs. I've gotten enough of it from him to last me for life, I assure you."

Leigh stirred and moved closer on the blanket. "Don't tell me you two are having trouble?" she said.

"Hasn't *he* told you?" Jennie said, more sharply than she had intended.

"Not at all," Leigh said. "As far as I've known, the only reason Brian's gone places without you was that you preferred to stay at home. My God, I've been thinking all this time that you two had the perfect marriage. I've always wanted to have that kind of an arrangement with Dirk. You know, he never goes away from the house and I like to go..." she waved one hand wide, "...everywhere."

"But you go," Jennie said.

Leigh sniffed. "Sure," she said. "And go through hell with him every time I get home. He doesn't trust me out of his sight." She sighed. "Or in it."

"She exaggerates a little," Dirk's mild tone cut down to them.

Both women started guiltily and turned to look up at the big man towering over them.

"Toss me that towel," he said to his wife.

She sat up and handed him a shaggy white towel. He took it and smoothed it over the crown of his bald head. He looked down at Jennie. "I hope you haven't been misled by all this prattle," he said easily. "I'm really a rather mild-tempered man."

She had thought so from the moment she had seen him. Yet now she was no longer sure. Surely the anguish in Leigh's words had been sincere.

"I'm sure you are," Jennie said half-heartedly. "But all women have to complain about their husbands now and then." She glanced sharply at Leigh. "We wouldn't be human if we didn't."

He pitched the towel at his wife's head in a gesture that was at once both playful and deeply affectionate. Leigh grinned back at him and moved over to make room for him on the blanket.

As she moved, Leigh's foot came into contact with Jennie's thigh. Jennie recoiled instantly, confused by their strange behavior, wary of Leigh's intentions.

"She's afraid of me," Leigh said to her husband. "What do you suppose is happening to my technique?"

Dirk laughed. "I've always told you you had a lousy one," he said.

If I had a grain of sense, Jennie thought, I'd get up and run like hell.

But she didn't move. Instead she glanced away to the water where Brian's blonde head moved slowly at a considerable distance from shore.

"Maybe she just doesn't like us," Leigh said.

She realized that the words were meant as a question. "Of course I like you," she said quickly. "I just don't …."

"You will," Leigh said. "Just give it time." She took a cigarette and let Dirk light it for her. She watched Jennie from behind a haze of smoke.

Jennie felt like she had forgotten every word she ever knew. Anyway, none of them would be sufficient to express what she was feeling. There could be no mistaking the intimation in the exchange between Leigh and her husband. She wasn't even sure there was a neat way out. But she'd find one.

"I … I think I'll go in for a swim," Jennie said, jumping up suddenly and dropping the robe onto the blanket. She couldn't just sit there, be stared at like a prize specimen on a pin. Even that cold, cold water …. Even Brian ….

She broke into a run, fleeing away from them as though for dear life. The sound of their laughter chased after her. At the water's edge she didn't hesitate, but took a deep breath and dove.

CHAPTER EIGHT

S he was running for her life, stumbling over the loose shale, picking herself up again and staggering on. Her hair hung loose around her shoulders, damp and stringy with perspiration. The muscles of her legs ached and an intolerable pain clutched at her right side. Still, she dared not slow down or even glance behind her for a sign of her pursuer. She heard loose stones skitter from under her feet, bounce over the precipice and into the water below.

She knew what he wanted, what they wanted. They wanted her to fulfill the promise made by the lewd portrait hanging in their library. They wanted her to prove she was the lusty, sensual girl in the painting and not the saintly fraud she seemed. She had tried to tell them that the painting was a lie. That she had never been the Jennie they wanted her to be. Never. Yet they didn't believe her. As Brian did not believe. As she was no longer really sure herself.

She was running downhill now, along the narrow path, her fingers sliding easily over the slick iron railing. Still they pursued her, shouting at her now. Calling her names she dared not listen to. Reminding her of Jake. Reminding her . . . .

She felt herself falling, clinging desperately to the railing that slid beneath her fingers like it had been coated with grease. Clinging, yet falling. Her feet going out from under her and her hands still grasping . . . .

She woke with a start that nearly pitched her out of bed. For a moment her fingers tightened convulsively on the fluted wooden pole supporting the canopy. She peered intently into the darkness, afraid still, listening for sounds of running feet somewhere near her.

Gradually her equilibrium returned, bringing with it a terror only slightly less real than that of her dream. She pushed herself away from the bed frame and into a sitting position on the edge of the mattress. Her toes poked beneath the bed for the pair of slippers she had forgotten to pack.

Foolish, she thought, to be afraid of the Whitmans. They certainly weren't the type to do anything against her will. They wouldn't force her to submit to them. Either of them—or both. And yet, she had sensed in their frank remarks down at the beach a determination not easily to be denied. Leigh had made it plain that they expected her to comply with their wishes. What had she said? *Give it time?*

Jennie felt as though her life amounted to a state of psychological warfare. She couldn't very well demand of Brian that he take her home before the expected end of their visit. If he listened to her at all, he would tell her she was being a damned fool. And maybe she was. Maybe.

She didn't believe it for a minute. She had no idea what kind of party games the Whitmans were used to indulging in, but she could guess, and she wanted no part in the whole business. Despite her behavior before her marriage, despite her fling with Jake, Jennie did not in any way consider herself a loose woman. A highly-practical one sometimes, but never indecent.

She padded barefoot into the bathroom, wondering how long she had slept since the party had finally adjourned after breakfast. She remembered that Brian had come upstairs with her. Had dropped his bathing trunks on the bedroom floor and wandered off for a shower. She had fallen asleep to the accompaniment of his bass rendering of something so off-key she hadn't been able to identify it. Where had he gone then? He certainly hadn't come to bed.

She stepped into the marble-tiled shower stall and began playing with the faucets. Too hot. Too cold. Too tepid. Freezing.... She gave up, finally deciding that the plumbing must have been imported along with the rest of the house. She worked the lavender-scented bar of soap into a lather on the cloth and moved it in slow circles on her body. The water was too cold to relax her, too warm to refresh her. It didn't even feel wet enough to get her clean.

She realized that she had a hangover and a lousy disposition to go with it. She'd had more than enough already of the old house and its weird inhabitants. Of Brian, too, for that matter. The way she felt right now, she wouldn't give a damn if she never saw him again.

Still, she was curious as to where he might have gone. Curious as people sometimes are out of habit rather than concern. It made little difference to her now what he did, she told herself, but, at least till tomorrow, she still had a right to know.

She stood on a fluffy, yellow bathmat, patting herself dry, feeling worse than she had before the shower, feeling exhausted and achy. Feeling even a little sorry for herself. In the cabinet she found a box of dusting powder, lavender-scented like the soap. She applied the puff energetically, sending a fine film of powder swirling around her to settle onto the bathmat. Pausing for a moment over her thighs, touching disapproving fingertips to the yellowish bruises Jake had left there. Even the thought of him sent a twist of anguish through her, a wrenching shame for what she had done. Not to Brian—he deserved anything he got—but to herself. For she understood now the warning her nightmare had implied. Understood that she could never again return to a life of sexual promiscuity. Once it had seemed like getting a lot for a little. Now it seemed like an impossible price to pay for practically nothing. She could manage by herself, with whatever alimony she could get out of Brian, with a job of her own. But she would never again bargain with her body for anything. Not for anything. Not if she starved.

Her frame took on a stance of determination, of pride. She stepped briskly into the bedroom, realizing suddenly that the place was as dark and gloomy as the middle of the night, though her senses told her it was barely midafternoon, Naked and barefoot, she padded the length of the room, pulling open shutters on the deepset windows, letting in a breath of fresh air and here and there a glimmer of light. She saw that the ivy that made the house almost tolerable to look at from the outside had choked off six of the tiny windows in the room, growing thick and untended like masses of matted hair. She remembered that Leigh had bragged that the house had been made livable and thanked heaven that she had not known the nut that Grandfather Whitman must have been. How could any man live in a dungeon like this? she wondered. Especially a man like Dirk, who took such pride in his physique and appeared to love the outdoors.

Busy disgruntling herself even further with her thoughts of the Whitmans, Jennie scarcely heard the low-pitched voice that drifted up to her from the terrace. She might have ignored it altogether. Except for the laugh that followed.

It was Brian's laugh, the special one he had when he had just heard a filthy joke. Or told one.

All of her leaned forward, alerted and tense. She could not see past the three foot thickness of the sill, could barely reach the sill at all. Quickly she dragged a velvet-covered chair over to the window and climbed up onto the seat. She leaned the palms of her hands on the sill, feeling the grime of old Scotland harsh against her skin. Still she could see nothing. The sound of Brian's laugh, lower now, more intimate, came to her again.

Grasping hold of a shutter, her bare feet aching on a rung of the chairback, Jennie managed to pull herself onto the deep but narrow sill. Her hips were too broad for the opening and she knelt there with her behind projecting into the room.

From her cranny, Jennie discovered a perfect view of the terrace and of the sea beyond. She had no fear of being seen, nestled there behind the ivy, and she leaned out as far as she could, looking for Brian and whoever might be with him.

She saw them, the two of them, side by side on a lounge the size of a bed and apparently used for the same purposes. Both were wearing sun glasses.

And nothing else.

Whatever else she thought about human nature, Jennie was ready to believe only one thing about a man and woman lying naked together. In the sun or anywhere else. Especially in the sun, she decided. The warmth did funny things to the body, gave it ideas it might never have had someplace else. She had discovered that for herself years ago, lying on a blanket in the sun, finding herself pressing hard against the packed sand.

She almost laughed to herself at the sight of her husband's body, flabby around the buttocks from too much city-living, starkly-white under the wiry black hair. He looked a little pathetic next to Leigh, with her golden tan and firm body. If he could see himself as she was seeing him, he'd run for his clothes.

But he wasn't seeing himself. He was seeing nothing but Leigh. He propped himself on one elbow and gestured with his other hand.

Jennie couldn't hear the words. But the sign language she understood very well. She watched Leigh's head tilt back and heard her laugh, low and privately.

With his free hand, Brian began to massage the back of Leigh's neck. She lay on her stomach with her head cradled on her arms, her face turned away from him. His hand moved from her neck, down her back, the strong fingers kneading along her spine. All the way down. His palm on her buttocks, her hip.

He put his arm across her back and drew her to him as he rolled over.

She pulled away from his kiss, laughing, and sat up, leaning stiff-armed against his chest. His hands grabbed her ribs and she leaned forward suddenly, nipping at the hair of his chest with her teeth.

Jennie smiled complacently. She doesn't want him, she thought. She's playing with him, kidding him along. Not like a woman does who wants a man. But the way she does if she doesn't care ... if she prefers women.

But there could be no doubt that Brian wanted her. Wanted her damned near any way he could get her. He moved her about, holding her tight with his hands on her hips.

Leigh leaned over and whispered into his ear. Jennie saw him nod. Leigh kissed him then, her mouth open, her tongue darting to meet his.

She rolled away from him onto her back. He moved with her, going onto his knees. Hunching over her, his mouth trailing along her belly.

Repelled yet fascinated nevertheless, Jennie watched as Leigh used her husband as she might have used another woman. Watched as he complied, willingly, to her demands. A feeling of nausea hit her stomach and she clung fast to the shutter, pressing herself together in the narrow confines of the window opening.

Leigh's body tensed, all of her arching upward. Her fingers tightened in Brian's hair. Wanting him to ....

He covered her completely and thrust at her furiously, lifting her with the strength of his passion.

Jennie's hand moved without her volition, cupping herself with the sweaty warmth of her palm. Her senses swayed, reeled to the rhythm of the figures on the lounge. She felt the tightening in her thighs, the quivering of nerves along her spine and down the backs of her legs.

Their bodies clung together in the convulsive motions of completion. Clung and then were still. Brian rolled onto his back, looking strangely overdressed in the sun glasses that still covered his eyes.

Jennie backed cautiously down from the ledge and leaned, panting and dripping with perspiration, against the wall. She felt drained of energy, weak in the knees and on the verge of tears. Her mind raged with confusion. And with something almost like fear.

It didn't really surprise her that Brian had done this thing to her. As angry and self-righteous as he had been feeling, he might even have done it in full view for her special benefit, wanting her to see.

But what about Leigh? And Dirk?

It was entirely possible that she had been wrong about Leigh. That the woman did indeed like men. And only men. It would certainly make more sense that way, considering that she had a husband. But if that were the case, how could she explain to herself the actions and words that Leigh had directed to her?

Jennie began to sense a creepy feeling that things in this house were not so simple as they might appear. She could accept perfectly well that Leigh might be attracted to Brian. Even Brian as he was now. She herself still felt the attraction strongly. And there was nothing especially peculiar about a woman going to bed with a man she found attractive. Not even, among the people they knew, if she happened to be married to someone else. It was not only accepted practice, but almost expected. Still, one didn't usually do that sort of thing . . . .

Jennie sighed, remembering her own experiences with Jake. Naked and anxious practically under Brian's nose. But Dirk Whitman was not a drunkard. And he certainly didn't seem the kind to encourage his wife's extramarital affairs.

Feeling a little steadier, Jennie turned to close the shutters she regretted having opened in the first place. She had always known about Brian's behavior. But she could have done very well without the first-hand experience. She rubbed her palms together, feeling the soot gritty and irritating against her flesh. She could do without another shower in that ancient bathroom, too. The feeling of filth and ugliness she had would take more than water to be dissolved. Bad enough that she had played the Peeping Tom. But her own response....

She shivered with disgust, remembering even now the hollow emptiness of self-inflicted satisfaction. She had been forced to it often, after the baby died. During the long months of her emotional recovery, her spiritual separation from her husband. Yet even necessity had not dulled the edge of regret, of guilt that assailed her conscience.

Heavily, she returned to the bathroom and began once more the hopeless process of reviving her nerves. She didn't want to see Brian again. Not ever. Whatever else she did this damned weekend, she must manage to stay out of his sight. For even though she could understand his behavior, perhaps even accept it, she despised him nevertheless. Hated him as only a woman undone can hate. She did not remember now her own experiences with Jake. Nor the long months of their misery together. She could remember nothing now but the sight of him, his hairy nakedness sprawling all over Leigh Whitman, devouring her with the force of his passion.

Even in memory, the sight of him sickened her. She rubbed the rough cloth briskly along her ribs, scrubbing ferociously, venting her anger and frustration on her own flesh. The tingling felt good, almost revived some of her energy. Still her head ached and the back of her neck felt as though someone had hacked at her with a mallet.

When she came into the bedroom, pushing a final pin into place in her still damp hair, she found Brian stretched out naked on the bed, his arms folded behind his head and a cigarette dangling from his lips.

Catching sight of him, she stopped abruptly, completely off-guard.

"You just wake up?" Brian said amiably.

So, Jennie thought. It must have been pretty good if he's even speaking to me.

"Not quite," she said crisply. Ignoring him, she went to the closet and took a pale blue linen skirt from its hanger.

"What's that supposed to mean?" he said around the smoke from his cigarette.

"Nothing," she said sharply, hearing the rise of tears in her voice.

She fastened the button at the waist of her skirt and stepped toward the bed to pick up her watch from the night table.

He leaned toward the table and dropped his cigarette into a glass ashtray. She felt his eyes boring into her, as though trying to see into her mind.

"I'm all right," she said impatiently. "Just leave me alone."

"Look at me," he said quietly.

She looked away.

He made a sudden grab for her wrist and pulled her sideways onto the bed. "I said, look at me, damn it."

She went limp, refusing to give him the satisfaction of a struggle.

For a moment he held her. Then, as suddenly as he had pulled her to him, he shoved her away.

Jennie stood up and straightened out her skirt. "Satisfied?"

"No," he said. "Should I be?"

"You ought to be," she said. "Tarzan."

He watched her narrowly.

She stepped away from him and made a quick check of her features in the glass. Taking a tissue from the box on the dresser, she dabbed at the right corner of her mouth. "You looked like a damned fool down there," she said over her shoulder, "with your bare ass hanging out like that."

She meant to hurt him, hurt him as much as she could. And he was pretty vain about his manhood.

But she hardly expected the reaction she got. She heard his feet hit the floor with a thud and before she could turn around, he was beside her, shaking her by the arm.

"Don't say that to me," he said, his tone a snarl. "Do you think I like it any better than you do?"

She stared at him, astonished. "Are you crazy? Let me go."

He let go of her arm and turned away from her. His shoulders drooped tiredly. "Go," he said disgustedly. "I wouldn't expect you to understand."

"Understand what?" she pleaded helplessly. "Understand what, Brian?"

He sat down on the edge of the bed. "Strings," he said. "Little strings with big nooses." He streached out on his back and closed his eyes.

She didn't know what the hell he was talking about. If anything. But, before she could ask him again, he had started to snore.

CHAPTER NINE

Standing in the center of the downstairs hall, Jennie strained her senses for an indication of human life. The old house, she had discovered, had a sound all its own. An eerie, echoing hollowness that rasped on the nerves. Despite the modern decor, the brightly colored wall hangings, she almost expected at any moment to hear a door creak open to reveal——

She heard the door open directly behind her, moving almost soundlessly on well-oiled hinges. She jumped involuntarily, startled half out of her wits.

"You'll be wanting some breakfast," a voice said inches from her shoulder.

Jennie spun around.

Arthur, still in the baggy dungarees that looked as though he had just come in from the garden, stood aloof, his ancient face wrinkled into a permanent leer. She had seen that face before, she thought, in horror films, on Halloween pranksters. It hadn't scared her then. But seeing it here, in this hellhole of a house, she felt terrified.

She put her hand to her throat, as though protecting herself from an attack. "Just some coffee," she said. "Please."

He moved off as soundlessly as he had come. The door clicked shut behind him.

When he had gone, Jennie breathed a sigh of relief. She felt like a damned fool, being scared of the ugly little man. If anything was out of kilter in this house, it probably wasn't Arthur.

Still, she could breathe much easier without him looking over her shoulder. She started down the long hall toward the terrace door.

On the threshold, she paused, not sure that she would be any better able to cope with Leigh than she had been with Arthur. A naked Leigh, at that. Nakedness had always made her vaguely uncomfortable. She was never quite sure where to look and had never managed to develop the aplomb to stare a naked body straight in the eyes.

She stepped out cautiously onto the terrace, peering around the edge of the heavy stone doorframe for sight of the woman.

Dirk's bald head above the back of the lounge looked somehow more obscene than Leigh's nakedness would have. Yet she was glad that the woman had vanished. Glad, too, that she had found Dirk waiting so conveniently. Despite the incident on the beach, she still felt safer with him than any of the others in this strange house. Including Brian, at the moment. Besides, if Leigh felt free to play games on the terrace with Brian, there was no reason in the world why she shouldn't feel just as free to have a little fun with Dirk. Not the whole way, she assured herself quickly. Just a mild flirtation to pass the miserable hours until they went back to the city.

"Hi, there," she called cheerily. Her heels clicked sharply against the flagstone.

Dirk's face poked out from the side of the chair. "Don't move another step," he said. "Just stand right there."

Jennie did as she was told, stopping in midstride and staring at the lounge curiously. The bald head had ducked out of sight. She saw the lounge rock a little with the movement of his body. A leg came into view over the side.

Jennie smiled to herself as he stood up and adjusted the waistline of his trunks. This was getting to be quite a show. And she wondered if Arthur, too, liked to trot around the house in the raw.

"You caught me…" he grinned, "…unprepared." He gestured toward the lounge, offering Jennie a seat on its comfortable foam rubber cushioning.

"I think I'll sit over here," Jennie said easily, approaching a wicker chair set back in the shadow of the house. "Out of the sun."

He inclined his head toward her. "Of course," he said. He stretched out on the lounge and crossed his legs at the ankles. "Have you had breakfast?"

"Arthur's bringing me some coffee," she said, wondering why he didn't hurry it up. She needed something to settle the nervousness quaking through her. She'd been through more already this afternoon than she usually encountered in a week.

"Good," he said. "Then I'd like to take you on a tour of the house. You haven't had that pleasure yet."

He said it casually. Yet something about the way he smiled with his eyes sent a tingle along Jennie's spine. She couldn't imagine what else might be in store for her and she was in no hurry to find out. She smiled brightly nevertheless, remembering her promise to herself of a mild flirtation with Dirk.

The way she felt now, it couldn't have been milder. "I'd love to see the place," she lied blithely. "It fascinates me. Especially the windows."

He glanced at her sharply, his eyes narrowed. "Why?"

"Why …." Confused by his sudden serious tone, she heard herself stammering and cut the words off sharply. She shrugged. "Just that I've never seen such thick walls," she said lightly. "I wonder the daylight ever gets in at all."

Dirk laughed, his face brightening instantly. "It doesn't," he said. "That's why we built the terrace. We practically live out here during the summer."

He is like a child, she thought. It's almost as though he has no control over his emotions at all. Raging one moment and grinning the next.

Uneasily, she turned her attention toward the sea and tried to appear absorbed in the contemplation of beauty. He didn't seem unbalanced, exactly. And yet, he didn't seem any too stable either. What were all those stories she had heard about inbreeding in wealthy families? The idiots and misfits it produced? If there were any truth to them at all, Dirk Whitman must indeed be living testimony. Not that there was anything specific you could put a finger on—you couldn't. That's what terrified her.

"Here's your coffee," Dirk said, breaking into her thoughts. He swung around on the lounge and pulled a low table between them.

He used his body beautifully, the smallest movement a study in grace. Yet the sight of his huge, hairless hands terrified her as much as his peculiar behavior. As she watched him pour coffee and send Arthur back for another pot, she found herself wondering, not about Dirk, but about Leigh. Leigh who lived with him and appeared so devoted. What sort of a creature must she be to have fallen in love with this man?

She took the cup he offered her and sipped slowly, finding a moment's protection from his interest. Still thinking about Leigh, she regarded him curiously from behind the cup.

"You're curious about me," he said, his tone neither angry nor complacent.

Caught off guard by his forthrightness, Jennie laughed. "Yes, I am," she admitted. "Terribly curious. I've never known anyone quite like you." She flushed. "I mean ...."

Dirk dispelled her embarrassment with a wave of his hand. "It's all right," he said. "I'm used to upsetting people." He patted the top of his head. "I lost all my hair," he explained, "after a bout of typhoid. And the size of me ..." he gestured with both hands down the length of his frame, "... runs in the family." He grinned. "I've been told I look like a eunuch with balls."

Jennie felt her cheeks flush hot with embarrassment. Yet she was relieved that he had considered her curiosity as applying only to his physical self. She had no desire to delve into the vagaries of his mind.

"Anything else?" he asked quietly.

"That'll do," Jennie said lightly. She finished the coffee and set the cup into its saucer. She heard the loud clatter it made and realized just how rattled she was. She couldn't just sit here with him, full of questions she hadn't the nerve to ask. She certainly had no intention left of pursuing a flirtation. Dirk Whitman in heat was an experience she could well do without.

She stood up without ceremony and extended her hand to Dirk. "I'm ready if you are," she said.

"Great," he said. He stood up and for a moment towered over her, staring at her intently. Then, apparently satisfied, he turned on his bare heel and stalked off toward the door of the house.

Jennie followed along dutifully from room to room, making the proper guestly remarks over cherished antique-marble tables, inlaid moldings, and bewhiskered ancestors. To her ultra-modern taste, the place looked like a mausoleum, complete with moldy corpses in wrapping sheets. The sheets, she discovered, were used merely to protect the furniture in unused rooms from becoming mildewed. The odor that reminded her of funerals and graveyards turned out to be a brand of incense that Leigh had gone wild about in Singapore. All through the house, they came upon trophies of Leigh's travels to hidden corners of the globe. But no mention was made of Dirk's part in these excursions.

"Don't you ever pick up souvenirs?" she asked curiously, fingering a handwoven wall-hanging from Turkey.

"Sure," he said. "We just haven't gotten to my collection yet."

"Of course," Jennie said, suddenly remembering. "Leigh told me you have a collection of antique cars."

Dirk threw back his head and laughed. The sound echoed hollowly in the high-ceilinged room. "That's a new one," he said, when he recovered his composure. "She usually says stamps."

She stared at him curiously, as confused and uncertain as she had ever been in her life. What had Brian dragged her into?

"Come on," he said, taking her arm. "I always save this for last."

He led her downstairs and out into the serving pantry behind the kitchen. Arthur watched them enter and cross to a thick, wooden door, set flush with the wall next to a fireplace. His eyes glittered with something close to terror and catching his expression, Jennie felt the gnawing fear she had known earlier.

"It looks like a secret passage," Dirk said. He hooked a finger into a loose piece of the molding. He turned to her and grinned as the door swung outward. "And it is."

She felt like she had just walked in on the second reel of a grade-Z movie, the way he stood aside and ushered her into the passageway with a wide sweep of his hand. Yet she sensed that he was merely playing a game, that he too felt like something in a movie rather than real life. She told him to go first and, relaxed now and curious, she followed after him.

They went down a long flight of steps and paused while he pushed open a heavy, wooden door. This one did indeed creak and Jennie laughed to herself, remembering the experience in the upper hall.

"How do you like it?" he said.

She heard the genuine pride in his voice and peered around him for a better view of the room.

The last time she had seen a collection like this one had been at Coney Island. Whips, racks, handcuffs set into the wall, the whole bit. Everything but the elephant crushing a man's skull with its foot. The barker at the side show had claimed that the finest collection of torture instruments in the world was housed inside. But obviously, he had never been in Dirk Whitman's cellar.

What intrigued her most was not the nature or even the extent of the collection. Men with lots of money and too much time on their hands did all kinds of strange things for kicks and who the hell was she to criticize Dirk's choice of pastime? But the condition of the equipment made her profoundly uneasy.

He led her down a short flight of steps and into the center of the room. Reaching out, he rubbed his palm along the well-oiled leather handle of a ten foot bull whip hanging from a stone post.

"Most of this stuff came with the house," he explained. "I've simply added to the collection."

"Your grandfather kept these things?" she said, feeling a little sick.

He turned to look at her directly. "Yes," he said. "My grandfather was an impotent, eccentric old man with young ideas. He used to hire sixteen-year-old girls to come out here and work for him and paid them enough to do anything he asked. And when he got too old to get aroused even by young girls, he started looking around for artificial stimulants." He gestured with a wide sweep of his arm. "This is what he came up with. Dad used to tell me stories about the old bird bringing women down here and putting them into chains and beating them. Or sometimes making them beat him."

"How awful," Jennie breathed, at once both horrified and intrigued. She'd heard a few stories of her own about sadists. But she had never been quite this close to the problem.

"Oh, I don't know," Dirk said easily. "It couldn't have done him any harm. He lived to the age of a hundred and three. And from what I've heard, he was still going strong a week before he died."

She looked at Dirk standing there, fondling the handle of the whip, his magnificent physique outlined sharply against the stark white walls of the basement. "You like the idea?"

He shrugged and let go of the whip. "Not for myself," he said. "I prefer ... something a little subtler."

Jennie suddenly lost all interest in asking questions. She started back toward the stairs to the first floor. "I think I could use that second cup of coffee now," she said.

Without comment, he followed her up the stairs and down the passageway into the pantry. As they came out, Arthur turned from the cupboard to watch them.

"Bring coffee out to the terrace," Dirk said to the old man.

She went out the side door and around the side of the house to the terrace. Settling herself on the uncomfortable wicker chair, she clasped her hands tightly in her lap, needing something to hang onto, yet not wanting to show her nervousness.

Dirk took his usual seat on the lounge, leaning back against the arm so that he could watch her face. "You didn't let me finish what I was saying."

"What?" Jennie blurted, knowing exactly what he meant, yet trying to hold it off as long as possible.

"About sexual excitation," he said patiently.

She leaned forward suddenly and reached for a cigarette, fumbling in the pack like she had a handful of thumbs.

Dirk snapped on the table lighter and held it toward her. "I have a fetish of my own," he said, "that would probably strike you as being almost as peculiar as Grandpa's."

She swallowed a mouthful of smoke and felt the tears start in her eyes. Maybe, if she kept her wits … "Oh?" she said, trying to stifle the anxiety in her tone.

He was gazing at her intently again, his eyes dark, little furrows of frown creasing his forehead. "Yes." He lowered his head slightly and the intensity in his stare increased.

She waited almost breathlessly, expecting him to go on with the speech, to tell her all the dark secrets that she didn't want to hear. She could have run. She could have screamed. But she sat frozen to her chair. Waiting.

Instead of going on, Dirk leaned back against the lounge and turned his face to the sun.

Jennie heaved a sigh of profound relief. For the moment, at least, she had been spared. She watched Arthur set the coffeepot down on the table and shuffle back into the house.

When he was out of sight, she leaned forward to the table and poured coffee for both of them, not wanting it now, not even sure she could swallow if she had to, but needing to keep herself occupied.

With Dirk's coffee cup in her hand, she glanced up.

He was leaning on his shoulders with his rear end up in the air, skinning the tight briefs over his thighs.

Whatever his secret evil, he must obviously have found time to enjoy it. Fascinated, she stared at him, unable to move, to glance away.

He lay back in the sunshine, enjoying with simple directness the sight of himself, the towering strength of his masculinity.

Very carefully, Jennie set the saucer down on the table. She pushed the chair away from her with the backs of her knees and tried to get up casually.

"Oh, don't go," he said, turning his head on his folded arms to look at her. "This is for your benefit."

"My ..." she choked on the words.

"Of course," he said simply.

It was almost too preposterous to be true. Almost. She had come downstairs ready to flirt with him, wile away the hours until she could get back to the city. But she hadn't done a damn thing. And he didn't even have the decency to seduce her.

"This is ridiculous," she said sharply. "What makes you think I'm the kind of woman ...."

"Every woman is that kind of woman," he said. "Even my beloved wife." He held out his hand. "Come here."

She took a step backward. "But I'm not interested," she blurted. "I ... What if Brian——"

He didn't let her finish anything. "Brian knows all about it," he said.

One of them must be going crazy. Even Brian . . . .

"What?" was all she could get out.

"Of course," Dirk said again. He sat up now and swung off the couch.

Too stunned to move, she let him take her arm and steer her onto the lounge. His movements were as graceful and beautiful as always. But there was nothing tender about the man. Nothing seductive. Suddenly Jennie understood what Brian had meant about the little strings with big nooses. Understood everything. Dirk, obviously, had allowed Brian use of the gallery in return for certain . . . considerations.

She could hardly blame Dirk for his attitude. He had paid for something and was intent on enjoying the merchandise. Brian, she hated already. With no one at whom to direct her hurt pride, her self-righteous venom, Jennie felt the strength go out of her. She lay back on the lounge and waited for Dirk to collect the debt Brian owed him.

Instead, he lay down beside her and took her hand in his. "Here," he said. He pressed the butt of her palm against him and forced her to massage him.

Never had she wanted anything less in her life, she told herself. Yet even as she said it, her body refused to believe her. She felt the quickening of his response. Felt the ache in her belly as her own flesh responded to the blatant sexuality of it. It wasn't Dirk she wanted. It wasn't love or tenderness either. But just plain sex, raw and simple, uncomplicated by the niceties of convention.

Her hand moved against him, more urgently now, almost desperately. Wanting it, wanting him, wanting him to . . . .

"Not that way," he said hoarsely. He gripped her shoulders and pulled her to him.

She felt his big hands pushing her, communicating the urgency of his need with the tight grasp of his fingers. Only for a moment did she hesitate. Lust raged through her. She didn't care if it was right or wrong. She didn't care . . . about anything. She only knew that her body screamed for fulfillment, driving her blindly, hurtling her forward along the shortest route. She went onto her knees, approaching him eagerly.

His satisfaction came almost instantly. She felt him heave convulsively, holding her tight with his legs.

He breathed a long sigh. "I've waited a long time for that," he murmured.

From the complete relaxation of his body, Jennie realized that she would have to wait a lot longer. But she didn't intend to let him get away with that. She'd had enough of that kind of crap with Jake. She moved herself along his body, writhing against him like a snake. Demanding that he respond to her, see her as a woman and not just a means to an end. Insisting with her breasts, her lips that he take her.

He sighed again.

She realized that he was asleep, konked out like a light. She stood up beside him and planted her hands on her hips, looking disgustedly at the hulk of a man who had failed her as completely as squat little Jake had done.

CHAPTER TEN

Her body aching with frustration, her pride more than a little battered, Jennie looked around for something to do that would help relieve the pressures building inside her. The way she felt now, she could swim from here to China or maybe hike all the way around the coast of Long Island. But whatever she did, she knew she needed to be in motion, going somewhere, doing something.

She strolled to the edge of the terrace and looked down over the stone barrier to the beach. In the light of late afternoon, the path looked more navigable than it had early in the morning with a head full of vodka. It still didn't appeal to her, but she didn't see that she had a hell of a lot of choice. If she hung around the house full of sleeping men, she'd probably wind up raping Arthur.

Taking a last glance at Dirk's reclining figure, she turned her attention to the winding path and started down. Before she had gone a dozen steps, the medium heeled shoes had already become a problem. She squatted by the path and pulled them off. If Leigh Whitman could do it, so could she. Or break her fool neck trying.

The smooth stone felt cool beneath her feet. Bits of gravel clung to her soles as she stepped cautiously along, clinging tightly to the railing with both hands.

Jennie had been around long enough, and in enough of the wrong places, not to waste time pouring solace into her punctured ego. She knew without having to be told that she was attractive to men. And women and children and animals. God knew, everywhere she went, somebody flipped over her. Even in the super market. If she wanted, she could have them lined up outside her bedroom door.

But that wasn't what she wanted, damn it. It wasn't at all—even if she had been acting that way. She wanted what every woman did. A husband, a home. Children, too, now that she was no longer afraid. But the husband came first in her head. Always. One man, to love and adore…and be faithful to. She couldn't help it if Brian acted like a pig.

And the others, she told herself, were no better. What kind of life could Leigh Whitman have with her husband? What could any woman expect from the likes of Jake Potter? Even for a woman who appreciated men as much as she did, Jennie realized, she had acquired in the past few days enough experience to sate her for a long time. Not enough satisfaction. Just enough experience.

Mumbling to herself, carrying a great burden of self-pity on her stooped shoulders, Jennie reached the bottom of the path and set out across the sand to the water's edge. After the gravel and stone, the sand felt good on her feet, still warm from the sun and powdery fine. She waded in up to her ankles, letting the gentle waves slide up her legs and ebb back to suck at the sand under her feet. Leaning down, she scooped water into her palms and playfully flung it away from her. She felt herself gradually beginning to relax, released now from the need to cope with people, with things. Alone by the sea, under the wide expanse of cloudless sky, Jennie let down the long mass of her hair and brushed it up and out with her hands, feeling freer than she had in years.

The water playing around her legs felt invitingly cool. She turned to look back up the long hill to the house, regretting that she hadn't thought to put on her bathing suit. She sighed, realizing that she would never have the energy to make the trip up and then back down again. She would just have to settle for wading.

Or would she? The thought hit her suddenly that this was hardly the place to worry about modesty. She had seen more nakedness in the past two hours than she'd had to contend with ever before in her life. Why should she be any different from the others?

She peered up and down the deserted beach. Not even a sandpiper disturbed the quiet surface of the sand. She raised her hand to shield her eyes from the sun and directed her glance out over the water. Some hundred yards from shore, a thirty foot cabin cruiser drifted idly at the end of a long mooring rope, hardly moving in the gentle swell of the waves. It looked completely deserted, like the beach.

Quickly she stepped out of her tight skirt and let it fall to the sand. Then the blouse and the slip. When she got down to the bra and panties, she suddenly lost her nerve.

Still wearing her underthings, Jennie ran into the shallow water and splashed out until it reached her waist. Then she took a deep breath and dove beneath the surface. The water closed over her and she let herself float without stroking, enjoying the icy coldness close to bottom. She had always been a strong swimmer, even though she had learned in city pools. Breaking clear of the surface, she struck out briskly, directing her course toward the cruiser. Wanting to lie on deck for a while, away from shore, away from the Whitmans. From Brian.

A three rung metal ladder fastened to the side of the boat offered easy access. She pulled herself up and swung onto the deck. Standing spread-legged to let the water drip from her, she fluffed out her hair to the afternoon sun. She tilted her head back and closed her eyes.

"I made you a drink," Leigh's voice said. "Vodka, right?"

Jennie lowered her arm stiffly, turning as she did so to watch the woman coming toward her from the cabin. Leigh was wearing a terry-cloth robe, pulled tight by a cord around her middle. As she stepped closer, Jennie remembered her own near-nakedness and crossed her arms over her breasts like a virgin taken by surprise.

Leigh appeared not to notice her discomfort. She held out the drink and shook it, jiggling the ice against the side of the glass.

Embarrassed by her own gaucherie and lack of ease, Jennie tried to emulate the woman's manner. Smiling a thank you, she took the glass and looked around for a place to sit down.

"Inside," Leigh said.

She turned to re-enter the cabin and Jennie obediently followed her inside. It was the only comfortable room she had seen since her arrival at the Whitman estate. Sighing gratefully for small favors, she dropped down lightly on a plastic-covered bunk against the wall and curled her legs up under her.

Leigh went to a cabinet at the foot of the bunk and dug out a huge, white towel. "Here," she said, tossing it to Jennie. "Don't sit around dripping. You might catch cold."

Jennie looked down at the drink in her hand, not fully understanding her hesitation, yet aware that she did not want to stand there and strip for Leigh's benefit. Not that it would make much difference after all she had been through already. She had certainly seen proof, with her own eyes, that Leigh liked men as much as any woman could. Besides which, the woman wasn't even looking at her. She had gone into the galley and Jennie heard her, rattling ice into a metal sink.

Taking advantage of the momentary privacy, Jennie rolled the wet panties down along her thighs and let them drop at her feet. Standing up, she stripped off the bra and reached for the towel. She bent over from the waist, sending her long hair flying in a cascade of damp strands. Briskly, she rubbed her scalp with the rough textured towel, then squeezed the moisture out of her hair.

She straightened up and swirled the hair back from her neck, fluffing it out behind with the towel.

"You know something?" Leigh's voice drawled behind her. "Your husband is a lousy artist."

Jennie stiffened involuntarily, recognizing a line when she heard it, even under the weirdest circumstances. Forcing herself to relax as best she could, she pasted a smile across her lips and turned to face Leigh. As she moved, she closed the towel around her and tucked one corner in between her breasts.

"Oh?" her voice lilted.

Leigh took her good time studying the figure before her, her glance roving slowly from head to toe and back again as though she were indeed inspecting a work of art. Jennie felt like Venus with arms, naked on a pedestal under the appraising eyes of the critics. Yet as long as Leigh gazed at her, she could not force herself to move, even to collapse onto the bunk directly behind her. It seemed almost as though a spell had been cast over the two of them, binding them together, to be held in the vise of mutual fascination.

For Jennie, returning the stare, was every bit as fascinated as Leigh. She had seen men aroused, often enough. Watched them perspiring and awkward in the simple mechanics of animal desire. But never had she observed a woman at first hand in the heat of passion. Certainly not one lusting after another woman. From her own experience, she understood that Leigh's response to her was quite different from a man's, even though it had the same object in mind. A kind of appreciation, of a desire to satisfy rather than to gain satisfaction that at once flattered and intrigued the object of her intentions. Jennie felt a strange twist of curiosity wrench through her, leaving her silent and immobile.

Leigh glanced away finally, breaking the spell, and sat down into a deck-chair opposite the bunk. She took a long drink from her glass and set it on a table at her elbow.

Jennie pulled the sarong tighter around her middle and fastened it securely. She lowered herself carefully onto the bunk, keeping her knees tightly together.

"He really is, you know," Leigh went on with the conversation as though there had been no break. "I thought that painting I bought was the sexiest thing in the whole world until I got a load of the real thing." She smiled. "I have suddenly become aware of his limitations."

Jennie understood all too well the intent of Leigh's speech. And she was just as well aware that she had no objection to the woman's flattery. Still, she had no intention of going beyond the flattery to something far less pleasant. She might just as well put a stop to the whole business right now.

"I thought you admired Brian's work," she said, her tone sternly serious. "You've given him a great deal of encouragement."

Leigh took her words as seriously as she had spoken them, turning off the debonair charm in her eyes and settling back against the chair. "I was tremendously impressed," she said, "by the portrait of you that's hanging in our library. So was Dirk. There's something about it that ...." She shrugged. "It's so damned sensual. What else can I say? Everyone who's seen it has fallen in love with you."

Jennie remembered all too well her own reaction to the painting. And "fallen in love" could hardly be an honest evaluation of the feelings the painting inspired. But it would be foolish to quibble with the woman over such an obvious point.

"And the rest?"

Leigh raised her shoulders in an exaggerated shrug.

The woman's nonchalance about something so important infuriated her. Even if she and Brian were through, she wanted to see him become successful. As she knew he deserved to be. Yet she could hardly be too annoyed with Leigh Whitman. She herself knew that Brian's work had deteriorated badly since the time he painted the portrait of her.

She kept her tone amiable. "If that's the way you feel about his work," she said slowly, "then why have you bothered to encourage him at all?"

Leigh spread her hands. "In the beginning, because of the portrait of you. I admired it and I bought it. I suppose buying a painting is a kind of encouragement."

Jennie smiled. "The only kind that really matters," she said.

Leigh nodded. "Well, then, you could say I encouraged him. After that, we kept bumping into each other at galleries and.... other places. We got along quite well. So ...."

Jennie realized that the smooth-tongued Leigh had begun stumbling over her words. Something about the woman's statements did not ring true. Sounded contrived. Designed, perhaps, to sooth a jealous wife?

"You don't have to worry about my feelings," she said honestly.

Leigh glanced at her curiously.

Jennie smiled complacently. "It's all right," she said. "I know about you and Brian." She raised her glass and drank deeply, keeping her glance averted from Leigh's.

"Oh?" Leigh breathed on a rising tone. "What do you know, Jennifer?"

She knew by the tone that Leigh was laughing at her. Triumphantly, perhaps, gloating over her success with Brian. Or perhaps it was something else. Perhaps she merely considered Jennie naïve and foolish. Whatever it was, Jennie hadn't the courage to face the woman. She held onto the glass tightly with both hands and propped it on her knees.

"Hey!" Leigh said. "You've got me all wrong."

When Jennie still refused to look at her, Leigh moved off the chair and squatted at Jennie's feet, her knees poking through the opening at the front of the robe. She peered intently into Jennie's face.

"Look at me, will you?"

Her tone was more kindly now, almost gentle. But if she had expected the nearness of her naked self to comfort and relax Jennie, she had made a miscalculation. Completely rattled now, Jennie raised the glass and drained its contents in breathless gulps.

Leigh took the glass as she lowered it and set it onto the floor. "You're being mighty stubborn, little girl," she said quietly.

"I'm not," Jennie blurted. "I know all about you, Leigh Whitman. I saw you on the terrace with … with my husband."

She tried to sound as self-righteous and injured as she had felt earlier. Yet the vodka played strange tricks with her empty stomach. She felt limp as an old dust-cloth. And almost as dirty. For here she was, defending the honor of her home and her marriage against the intruder, and feeling sensations very unbecoming to a devoted wife. The frustration of her assault upon herself, of the abortive affair with Dirk rushed in on her, leaving her dull and defenseless, yet blazingly alive in the way she least wanted to be.

Leigh made no attempt to touch her. Yet Jennie knew that it would not be long. Knew it … and wanted it. Realizing that she wanted it, could not accept her own desire. The tears welled up in her eyes, tears of guilt and confusion.

Leigh put her hand on Jennie's knee and shook her gently. "Look at me," she insisted.

Jennie blinked away the scattering of tears and bit hard on her lip. She forced herself to face Leigh's searching glance.

Yet, when Jennie faced her, Leigh glanced away. "I don't know how to make you understand," she said. "Yes, I was on the terrace with Brian. But it means nothing, Jennifer. I——"

"Means nothing?" Jennie said sharply. "Maybe it means nothing to you. But——"

"I didn't mean it that way," Leigh interrupted her. "Of course it means something. Everything means *something*. But I'm not interested in Brian. It had nothing to do with …." She broke off and shrugged. She pushed her palm against Jennie's knee and started to rise. "Forget it," she said crisply.

Jennie grabbed her wrist. Her alcohol-fogged brain whirled with confusion. "Tell me, Leigh," she murmured. "Please tell me."

Jennie heard the insistence in her tone. If Jake had been here, he would have laughed, she thought. Talk about corny dialogue! Maybe she didn't know anything about Leigh Whitman's private life. But she sure as hell understood the drift of their conversation. It was one of the oldest and tiredest lines in existence. And she didn't care. She didn't give a damn what approach the woman used. Just so she got where she was going. Just so ....

"It's you I want, Jennifer," Leigh said in a hushed tone. She glanced away. "I've been in love with you ever since ...." Now she looked up and met Jennie's eyes. "Ever since I saw the painting, I guess."

Jennie grinned triumphantly. "Your husband's right," she said confidently. "You have got a lousy technique."

Leigh nearly fell over backwards. "What?"

Jennie rested her palm on the hand Leigh still had on her knee. "I have a very wise friend," she said huskily, "who taught me never to waste time on talk." She patted Leigh's hand. "You're not in love with me, any more than I'm in love with you." She heard the alcohol thickening her tongue, as it had already blurred her thinking. But she had gone too far to stop now. And she intended to go further. "But we both want something, Leigh. So ...." She shrugged, feeling cocky and terribly sophisticated.

"Jesus Christ," Leigh breathed.

Just like it was with Jake, Jennie thought. Only better. Much better.

The way Jennie felt, she was ready for anything. Instantly, with none of this fooling around. She didn't care about convention. She didn't care about pretensions and niceties. She didn't feel nice. Just hot. Just alive all over and aching for the touch of another human being. Her body one great womb, willing and waiting, ready to swallow up the universe in its greed. Ready to devour and destroy.

But Leigh had other ideas. She didn't seem to be in a rush at all. She came out of her squat slowly, her long, gentle fingers caressing the inside of Jennie's thigh, moving up under the towel as she maneuvered onto the bunk beside her. She bent her head, seeking the warm cleavage, her tongue moving against Jennie's flesh.

Jennie herself unfastened the towel from around her body. Unfastened it and arched her body to meet Leigh's roving lips.

Just as eagerly, Leigh untied the sash of her robe and let the bulky terry cloth drop to the floor. She put her arms around Jennie and kissed her full on the mouth, her own open, her tongue darting between Jennie's lips.

Jennie felt her back touch the cool plastic seat. Yet nothing would have felt cool now. Her flesh flamed at Leigh's touch. And Leigh touched her ....

Leigh's mouth circled on her breasts, teasing. Teasing. Sending quivers of sensation through her that were almost painful in their intensity. She felt the woman's own breasts, small and firm yet taut-pointed in desire, against her lower belly. Her hips rotated slowly, relishing the touch of Leigh's body.

Leigh obliged willingly, pressing herself hard against Jennie. Using her hands, her breasts, her mouth. Massaging her gently, yet urgently, demandingly.

Jennie arched her back, pressing herself upward off the bunk. The pain of it had become almost unbearable. Almost, yet maddening in its promise. She wanted more. She wanted everything. And all at once. She needed fulfillment. And yet she needed this as much. The sheer ecstasy, the pure sensuality of a body completely aroused. And if it lasted forever, it would be over too soon.

Yet, when it happened, she forgot about time, about eternity. The moment was now. And the moment was timeless. She soared dizzily, seeking her orbit, hurtling through nothingness. A bodiless, weightless soul achieving momentary union with its god.

And then, peace. Complete quiet in the aftermath of violence. She lay on the narrow bunk staring at the ceiling, feeling a sense of release and fulfillment more complete than any she had known since .... since the good days with Brian. But even in the midst of her pleasure, she knew a moment of pain. Of emptiness. And she almost hated Leigh, hated her for being a fraud, for not being a man. For not being Brian.

Yet it was not Leigh whom she should hate, she knew. Leigh had done the best she could, with what the good Lord gave her. And she had satisfied Jennie almost completely. Physically, at least, the fulfillment had been perfect. It was the other part that felt empty. And in her heart Jennie knew that no one but Brian had ever even come close to that.

She put her hand gently on Leigh's head, resting against her hip.

Leigh moved up and leaned on one arm, smiling down at her. She put a finger under Jennie's chin and tilted her head back. "Dirk will hate me for that," she murmured.

Jennie opened her mouth to speak, but Leigh cut her off with a kiss. Even in the near-apathy of completion, her body began to respond. She forgot Dirk. Even forgot Brian. Forgot everything but the need to satisfy her craving. To render herself senseless with lust so that she could forget.

"Take me," she murmured. "Take me."

And Leigh moved to comply.

CHAPTER ELEVEN

Jennie awoke feeling cramped and stiff, lying on her side on the narrow bunk with Leigh beside her. Outside it was already daylight, the sun beating hotly through the portholes of the cabin and grating against her eyelids. The plastic seat-cover felt sticky and intolerably warm to her touch. She shifted slightly, but could not move Leigh off her shoulder without waking her.

Neither of them had gotten much sleep during the late afternoon and long night. They had responded to each other like two starved souls, each demanding satisfaction again and again. She had needed Leigh, had needed someone whose needs were as desperate, as insatiable as her own. It did not bother her, in the conventional sense, that Leigh was a woman. She had never been that kind of a prude about sex. But it did bother her, as she had known it would, that Leigh was not a man. For all their blatant enjoyment of their hours together, Jennie still felt a nagging emptiness, a lonesomeness that left her irritable and unsatisfied.

She lay on her back, staring out the porthole beside the bunk, waiting for Leigh to awaken. She would have to let the woman know, somehow, that this had been it for them. A wonderful night of passion that must not be repeated. For herself, she knew that she and Brian were through. Hopelessly through. But there was still Jake. And others. Many others. For Leigh, there was Dirk...as there must always have been Dirk. Often during the night she had remembered Leigh's words: "Dirk will hate me for that." And she felt that she had understood the anguish in the woman's soul. If as it now appeared, Leigh had promised Dirk never to give in to her desire for a woman, he must indeed hate her for that—for Jennie, and for God only knew how many other misadventures. Whatever her reasons for remaining married to him, Leigh obviously wanted to maintain her relationship with Dirk.

Her mind filled with confusion, Jennie half turned her head to peer at the face so close to hers.

Leigh's eyes were open and smiling, soft with something Jennie wanted no part of now. She hated to love and run. It wasn't very nice at all. Yet ....

Leigh kissed her tenderly on the point of her chin. "You know something," she said. "You didn't want to hear it last night. But I am in love with you."

Jennie could have cried. Somehow, she could believe Leigh now. But in accepting the truth, she could feel only sad. Not that she didn't like the woman. She did. As much as she could like any woman. But love?

Leigh sighed. "That's the way the rocks pile," she said flipply. She crawled over Jennie and stood up. "I'll make some coffee."

Jennie let her go, knowing that the woman understood her feelings without having to be told. Knowing, too, there was nothing she could say in honesty to ease the woman's hurt. She reached for Leigh's robe where she had left it on the floor and slipped it on, tying the sash tight around her middle. No use aggravating the situation. If she didn't want to arouse the woman, the least she could do was cover up the bait.

Leigh brought steaming cups of instant coffee and set them on the low table. She pulled the table in front of the bunk and sat down beside Jennie, keeping her attention centered on the domestic task.

Jennie sipped slowly at the tasteless hot brew, wishing she had a cup of real coffee to soothe her ruffled nerves, yet deriving strength from the scalding liquid nevertheless. She knew Leigh well enough by now to realize the woman's weaknesses. She understood that Leigh would not make an issue of her rejection, yet this did not ease her own conscience and Jennie felt herself wanting to make an issue of the thing. Wanting to drag it out and chew it over—hoping to find something for which she could blame Leigh, blame anyone but herself.

"Leigh, I'm sorry all this happened," she began slowly. It wasn't what she had wanted to say. Yet it was said. Quickly, she went on. "I mean, I know it was all my fault. I practically raped you last night." She gestured distractedly. "Oh, I was a little high. But I damned well knew what I was doing and...."

Leigh put her forefinger over Jennie's lips. "Don't say it," she warned. "You'll only give us both a headache."

"But..." Jennie mumbled.

"Shh!" Leigh said. "We both had a ball last night." She shrugged. "So let's let it go at that."

Jennie smiled at the woman gratefully. She knew by the expression in Leigh's eyes that the woman would not let it go in her mind for a long time. But there would be nothing else between them. That way. Just friendship and a mutual affection, and she could use a friend right now.

She faced Leigh squarely. "May I ask you something?"

"Of course."

Jennie lowered her glance, feeling suddenly embarrassed and not at all sure of herself. "It's about Brian," she muttered.

"I thought as much," Leigh said easily. "Ask away."

She bit her lip to stop the rush of foolish words tumbling to her lips, the anguish and the agony of their lives together during the past two years. She could spare Leigh that. Could spare herself now. She took a deep breath and looked straight into the woman's eyes. "How long have you been having an affair with Brian?"

She had expected almost anything. Denials, protestations, guilt. Anything but Leigh's hearty, deep-throated laugh. Her nostrils tightened indignantly.

"I'm sorry," Leigh gasped. She patted Jennie's hand. "You don't understand at all, do you?"

"What?"

Leigh glanced away from her. "It doesn't matter," she said. "Now."

My God, Jennie thought. Here we go with the riddles again. Every time I ask a sensible question ....

"That was the first time," Leigh said, interrupting Jennie's blossoming self-pity. "And the last."

Jennie stared at her for a long moment, remembering the complete abandon, the unselfconsciousness of the naked bodies on the lounge. "I don't believe you," she said finally.

Leigh shrugged. "That, as they say, is your problem. But I can tell you, my naïve little girl, that I have no interest whatsoever in your husband. In my own, yes. And in you. But in Brian?" She grinned. "I don't mean to insult either of you, my love, but he's just not my speed."

Jennie felt like she was losing what little was left of her mind. If the woman had no interest in Brian, then how could one account for the scene on the terrace? And if she did, why bother trying to lie her way out of it now?

But before she could throw more questions at Leigh, the woman had stood up and cleared away the coffee cups. She came back from the galley and leaned against the cabin wall. "If you're ready," she said, "we'd better go back to the house, before they call out the cops."

Jennie shed the robe as she stood up and stepped into the still damp panties. Leigh stood waiting as she fastened her bra. Then the woman turned on her heel and went outside.

By the time Jennie reached the deck, Leigh had already dived over the side. Jennie followed her in. She struck out strongly for shore, keeping the bobbing head in view, yet watching the distance widen steadily between them.

She stood up in shallow water and waded the rest of the way ashore. Leigh sprawled naked on the sand, watching her with an amused expression on her face and waiting.

Jennie noted the expression and frowned. "What's funny now?" she said sharply, still stinging from Leigh's dismissal of her as a naïve child.

Leigh gestured across the sand. "You forgot about the tide," she said calmly. "You'll have to arrive home in your BVD's."

Jennie's hand flew to her throat. She had indeed forgotten. At the time when she had gone in for a dip, there had been no need to think about it, yet, standing here in her lace-edged panties and the tight bra, she felt like a spectacle. If Brian were watching, he wouldn't have to be told what had happened. Leigh in her stark nakedness was enough to attest to that.

Still smiling, Leigh bounded up from the sand and set off for the path up the hill.

Jennie had no choice but to follow. They didn't bother trying to make conversation and Jennie thanked God that the steep pathway demanded all her concentration. What they must look like! She kept her attention riveted to the rocks, as though obliterating the sight of the two of them by refusing to look upon it. Near the top, where she had left them, she retrieved her shoes and slipped them on. Her feet were swollen with the heat, gritty with sand and her shoes rubbed painfully against the skin.

Stepping at last onto the terrace, she drew a sigh of relief and raised her glance.

Leaning over the barricade about fifty feet away, a spyglass trained on her near-nakedness, Dirk Whitman looked like a little boy leering at the old maid across the street. Involuntarily, she crossed her arms on her breasts, hiding as much as she could without looking absurd.

"Don't bother," Leigh said. "He's had a good look already."

Remembering suddenly her session with Dirk on the lounge, Jennie realized that it was a little late to be a prude. She let her hands fall to her sides. "I suppose you're right," she sighed.

"Oh, oh!" Leigh breathed.

Jennie stiffened at her tone, knowing without moving her head what Leigh had seen.

"We've had it, chick," Leigh said gently. "The irate husband is about to bust a stitch."

She followed the line of Leigh's vision and watched Brian emerge onto the terrace. Haggard and hollow-eyed, he looked as though he hadn't slept in a week. Yet he had been asleep when she left him. Sleeping soundly. He must have spent the night drinking, sopping his ego with alcohol in an effort not to think about her. He looked drunk now.

Yet, as he came closer, Jennie knew that Brian had probably never been more sober in his life. If he had had anything at all to drink, it had turned to gall, to poison in his system, filling him with hatred for her. Hatred and a need for revenge.

He didn't even see Leigh. Or Dirk. He stalked across the terrace directly toward her, murder in his eyes and the set of his jaw. His hand went back, then shot out at her.

The blow glanced off the side of her cheek. She reeled backwards, clutching at the stone barricade for support. Gasping for breath, tears flowing freely down her cheeks.

Dirk was at Brian's side almost instantly, grabbing him by the arm and spinning him away from Jennie. "Take it easy," Dirk rasped hoarsely, "or I'll throw you over the side."

Even in his murderous rage, Brian realized that he was no match for this giant of a man. His fists clenched and unclenched convulsively, yet he made no move to break away.

Dirk shoved him away disgustedly. "You haven't got the guts to hit a man," he said.

The animosity between them that had lain dormant under the guise of civilized acceptance now blazed openly on the faces of both. Jennie glanced from one to the other, expecting blood-shed at the least, perhaps even worse. Wanting Brian to stand up to Dirk, to defend his manhood and his pride. Yet knowing even before he turned away that Brian would not.

Dirk looked at his wife. "There's coffee," he said tiredly.

"Let me get some clothes on," Leigh answered him, not meeting his glance, but watching Brian.

He leaned both fists on the stone barricade and bent forward, his head bowed, shoulders drooping. Seeing him like this, defeated and stripped bare of all pride, Jennie both despised and pitied him. But at the moment she felt nothing even resembling love. She could never pity and love him at the same time. Helplessly, miserably, she glanced at Leigh, looking for help.

Dirk stepped between them and rested his hands on Jennie's shoulders. There was something protective and almost fatherly about his calm strength. She peered into his face anxiously.

"It's all right," Dirk said easily. "You may stay here with us for as long as you like." He tilted his head and glanced at her quizzically. "Unless you intend to go back with him?"

Jennie shook her head vigorously. "No," she said. "Not now. Not after . . . ."

He squeezed her shoulders reassuringly. "I understand," he said. "Leigh's already mentioned that the two of you hadn't been getting along." He nodded at Brian's back. "Which isn't difficult to believe after this little episode."

He stepped away from her and reached out to take his wife's arm. Leigh's eyebrows arched slightly, but she said nothing.

Dirk bent to plant a kiss on the end of his wife's nose. "It's all right, darling," he said softly. "We both made fools of ourselves this time."

Jennie watched them walk off together, Dirk with his arm around Leigh's shoulder, Leigh with her arm around Dirk's hips. Indeed, they had all made fools of themselves this time. All four of them. Yet for the Whitmans, she realized, there would be no problem. A slight ripple on the smooth surface of their marriage. But no tidal wave, no hurricanes.

But for herself . . . . She looked at Brian, feeling sad and utterly hopeless. Too much had gone before to allow either of them to accept the other, too much and too little. The utter futility of their situation settled over her like a suffocating hand. She couldn't even find anything to say.

They remained for a long while, somber and silent, each wrapped in his own pall of misery. Finally Brian moved and turned slowly to face her.

The expression in his eyes made her feel sick to her stomach. How could any man have come to this? Even Brian? She had known his lack of courage, his inability to cope. But she had not known this complete acceptance of failure. And though he slumped only slightly, he looked to her like a scarecrow, spineless and wobbly-legged.

"So we're finished," he said dully.

Jennie could have laughed in his face. Even with her he couldn't be a man. "You made that clear before we got here," she said crisply. "You told me you'd already been to the lawyer."

He grunted. "I have," he said.

"Well, what did you expect me to do, sit around on my hands and wait for you to say the word?"

"But a woman, for chrissake. Why a woman, Jen?"

"Why not?" she snapped. "You did."

He slammed his fist angrily against the barricade. "What the hell's the matter with you?" he raged. "I've never heard anything that stupid out of you before and I've heard plenty."

She felt curiously detached from his rage, as though she were watching the two of them from a distance, laughing at the pettiness, the futility of their plight. "I don't think it's so stupid," she said calmly. "I enjoyed every minute of it. And so did you." She laughed. "Maybe you're just jealous?"

He raised his hand and balled it into a fist. But this time he shoved it into his jacket pocket instead of slashing out at her. "You're a damned fool," he said harshly. "If you had any sense, you'd know damned well why I did it."

"Oh, I know all right," Jennie said smugly. "You've had hot pants for Leigh Whitman ever since you met her."

Brian sighed tiredly. "It doesn't matter," he said. He shook his head, as though clearing away the confusion inside it. "But I'm not leaving you here, Jennifer. For your own good. I want you to come back to the city with me. Right now. We'll straighten this mess out after we've had time to simmer down a little bit."

"You want..." she gasped. "I wouldn't go anywhere with you after...." She gestured angrily, wanting him to feel her disgust and disappointment. "And what's more, I'm not simmering at all, if that's what you think."

He grabbed her suddenly by the shoulders and pulled her to him roughly. "God damn you," he rasped. His lips sought hers fiercely, demandingly. His arms tightened around her, pressing her hard against him.

She felt as if the breath had been knocked out of her. For the first time in the years she had known him, her body did not respond eagerly to his touch. Fury flamed through her, stiffening her body, drawing her away from his grasp. Her teeth went into his lip.

He spun away from her, the back of his hand pressed against his lip. She saw a trickle of blood seep down his chin.

Horrified at what she had done, Jennie waited for him to kill her quick and get it over with. She closed her eyes and tilted her head back, hardly daring to breathe.

"I deserved that," he said quietly. He took a step toward her, but made no move to touch her.

She opened her eyes and looked him straight in the face. "Who's the fool now?" she said.

He took a deep breath and let it out slowly. "Okay," he said. "For the last time, what's it going to be, Jennifer? Heads or tails?"

She deserved at least that much snideness from him and probably a lot more. But she'd be damned before she'd let him have the last word. Inclining her head, she smiled, very sweetly. "I can have either I want," she said. "Right here."

She turned on her heel and started toward the house. Dirk came out alone as she approached.

"I'm taking you up on the invitation," she said cheerily. "At least for a while."

"Brian's leaving?"

"Hmm," she murmured. "It's all finished between us, except for the alimony." She tried to keep her tone light. Tried hard. But somewhere deep inside her, she was crying. Unsure even now of her feelings.

Dirk grinned broadly, his childlike face wrinkling around the mouth and eyes. "Great," he said. He turned toward Brian and called out to him, "I'll have Arthur drive you in."

Brian came toward them, his face deathly pale. His eyes narrowed as he met Dirk's glance. "Thanks," he said. "And Dirk ...."

"Yes?"

"You can take your goddamned gallery," Brian said, "and shove it." He stalked away from them and around the side of the house.

CHAPTER TWELVE

An air of quiet settled over the house immediately Brian had gone. Alone in her room, Jennie had listened to the sound of the big Lincoln on the gravel drive, feeling both sad and relieved that the moment of their separation had finally come. They would both be better off without each other, she told herself. Yet Brian's last words had startled her. Startled and frightened her, too. Without Leigh and Dirk Whitman's support, Brian Dunbar might easily become just another Village bum, painting and whoring between bottles, barely managing to keep himself alive.

He would have to sell the house. Though there wouldn't be much left after the debts were paid. Jake would help him. If he'd still have anything to do with Jake.

The troubled thoughts skittered across her brain, bumping into each other like a handful of marbles in a box. I'm tired, she thought. Just plain tired. And I can't think about this now. I can't. Maybe tomorrow. Maybe next week. Maybe ....

She settled back against the pillows on the too-empty bed and let herself drift into a deep sleep.

She awoke with a start and sat bolt upright in bed. She felt as though she had just dozed off. Yet the long shadows across the carpeted floor told her that she had slept for many hours. She listened attentively, seeking the sound that had brought her awake.

"Hi, there, sleepyhead," Leigh said, coming toward her soundlessly on bare feet.

She had clothes on this time, Jennie noticed with relief. Not what you'd call ample covering for a social occasion. Just enough to be indecent. Her bright blue bikini was even skimpier than the one her husband wore and almost as intriguing.

Jennie sighed and stretched luxuriously. "What time is it?" she asked.

Leigh stopped a full yard away from the bed, but her glance leaped right in under the sheet. "Four o'clock," she said.

Jennie pulled the sheet up higher around her breasts. "I suppose I ought to get up."

Leigh laughed deep in her throat. "Would you like me to turn my back?"

Jennie had to laugh, too, realizing how ridiculous she must appear after the acrobatics of last night. She pushed the sheet aside and stood up close to Leigh. She had, after all, thrown herself on the hospitality of the house.

Leigh's hands cupped her breasts and squeezed them together. She bent her head and pressed her lips gently to the warm flesh. Then, as suddenly, she stepped away and gave Jennie a shove on the behind. "Put something over those things," she said. "We're going on a picnic."

"Oh?" Jennie breathed, hoping that Leigh meant the two of them. Alone. She wasn't ready yet to cope with Dirk. The experience must have been as embarrassing for him as it had been for her.

Or had it?

"Um hmm," Leigh replied. "For some insane reason, Dirk seems to think nothing would please you better than a picnic on the beach." She grinned. "I could think of a couple of things that would be a lot more exciting. But..." she raised her shoulders in a look of exasperation.

Jennie flushed, both embarrassed and pleased by Leigh's treatment of her. Apparently the woman had decided to claim Jennie as her own, now that Brian was out of the way. And if she wanted it that way.... Why not? Jennie thought. A rejection now would ring hollow to anyone's ears.

She stepped to the dresser and pulled out the top drawer. Inside, her things lay in a jumbled heap, mute testimony to Brian's frenzied hurry to get away from the house. She moved them about listlessly, straightening a pile of undies, not having the energy to be bothered. Even now that he had gone, Brian was still there to remind her of her failure—of their failure together. The taste of it lay bitter in her mouth.

Leigh leaned around her and picked a bright yellow and red kerchief from the mess. "Here," she said. "Wear this."

"Wear it?" Jennie squealed. "It's not big enough to …."

"Oh, yes it is," Leigh said. "Just watch." She laid the kerchief on top of the dresser and folded it into a neat triangle. Holding it by two corners, she put the long side around Jennie's middle and knotted it in front. Then she pulled the other corner between her legs like a diaper and tied it fast.

"There," she said triumphantly. She stepped back and admired her handiwork. "What's wrong with that?"

"I wouldn't be caught dead this way," Jennie breathed. She glanced into the mirror. It didn't look half bad at all, she decided. In fact ….

"What about the top?" she said.

Leigh laughed. "See? It's not a thing to be caught dead in. But alive, baby, you'll do very well." She rooted in the dresser drawer and pulled out a black satin bra. "How about this?"

Jennie took the bra and slipped the straps over her arms. She lifted one breast, then the other into its cup.

Leigh moved in close and put her arms around Jennie to hook the bra. When she had fastened it, she stood there for a moment, holding Jennie against her. Then, as she had before, she stepped suddenly away. "Come on," she said. "Dirk's downstairs, waiting for us."

Her reluctance to face Dirk waned before the rush of curiosity concerning Leigh's behavior. Ardent and tender one moment, withdrawn and flippant the next. It was obvious to Jennie that the woman's desire had not abated at all. Yet something held her back. It was almost as though she were afraid. Jennie wondered what kind of scene the woman had had with her husband. If he had threatened her with .... With what? Even that eluded her.

Following Leigh downstairs, Jennie's mind hummed with questions, trying to unravel the mystery of the relationship between Leigh Whitman and her husband. But, no matter which way her intuition led her, she came up with nothing but a blank.

Dirk jumped up from the lounge and came forward eagerly to greet them. He took Jennie's hand and held it between his own. "You slept well?"

"Very," Jennie said, wishing he would let go of her hand. She didn't want him to touch her. Not at all. "I feel much better now."

"Good," he said. "Leigh told you .... "

"Yes," Jennie said. She smiled. "And I'd love to go on a picnic." The nearness of him began to rattle her. She felt the smile grow stiff and unnatural on her lips.

He squeezed her hand, then let it go. Turning toward the house, he shouted for Arthur. In a moment the old man toddled out onto the terrace carrying a wicker basket so heavy that it threw his weight off balance.

Dirk took the basket in one hand and swung it easily onto his broad shoulder. "Let's go," he said. And almost before the words were out of his mouth, he was striding toward the edge of the terrace and the winding path down to the beach.

Jennie sighed and set off behind him with Leigh at her heels. Why in the hell don't they have an elevator? she thought irritably. With all their money, this desire for primitive living seemed an absurd affectation. No one in his right mind could enjoy hiking up and down that damned hill.

Yet she went uncomplainingly, trailing after Dirk, who moved down as easily as though he were gliding across a dance floor. When he reached the bottom, he didn't bother waiting for

the women, but set out at a trot across the sand, the basket swinging from his hand.

He set the basket on the sand beside a deep pit and went off
in search of drift wood. He had disappeared from sight by the
time Jennie and Leigh reached the picnic site.

"We might as well make like home," Leigh said. She squatted
on the sand and lifted one side of the hinged lid. She extracted
first a dark-green blanket and tossed it at Jennie's feet. "For you."

Jennie shook out the blanket as best she could, smoothing
the corners carefully and setting a small stone on each to hold it
in place. She took plates and napkins and parcels of food as Leigh
handed them to her and found a place for them on the blanket. It
looked like a banquet for twenty. But she had seen Dirk's appetite
in action at dinner on Friday evening.

Dirk came over a sand dune directly behind them and
dropped an armload of wood beside the pit. Looking up at him,
it struck Jennie that he looked more like a child now than ever—a
kid auditioning for the cub scouts. He went down on his knees,
laying small sticks and a handful of crumpled paper into the pit,
then building up a mound of the driest bits of driftwood. When
he had arranged the pyre to perfection, he took a match from
Leigh and touched it to the edge of the paper. The fire sputtered
for a moment, then caught and flared.

He stood up, dusting his hands on the behind of his trunks.
Jennie found herself wondering if there were enough material
there to do him any good. The black trunks he wore now were
little more than a sharkskin G-string.

"That does it," he said unnecessarily. He nodded to Leigh.
"The rest is up to you."

"It always is," Leigh said.

Both Dirk and Jennie glanced at her sharply. Ignoring them,
Leigh got down to business, pushing hot dogs onto the long
prongs of a fork.

They made an elaborate affair of their meal, drawing it out for hours, breaking off once for a swim in the cold water and coming back to lie exhausted for a few minutes, then eat again. Jennie felt about ready to burst, yet something about the sea air, the quiet of early evening with the fire already burning down to embers, relaxed and soothed her, allowing her thoughts to drift idly in a haze of unreality.

She found that she was thinking again about Brian. As, inevitably, she always thought of him. Not Brian as he had become, married to her. But Brian as she had dreamed of him, in the early years of their marriage. Things could have been so different for them—indeed should have been so different. If they had had money, even a little, if they could have afforded a place at the shore, even a little place.... Most of all, if they could have had children. If their son had lived.

She lay back on the blanket and closed her eyes, watching in her mind the long succession of *ifs* stretch out in an unending string. A long, long string with a noose at the other end. Tears welled up in the corners of her eyes and she felt too warm and nearly ill with the weight of her unhappiness.

She felt Leigh stir beside her, lean above her, touching the side of Jennie's arm with her breast.

"What's the matter, kitten?" Leigh murmured. "The world too much for you?"

For a long moment, Jennie managed to hold it in, the aching pain and the misery. In front of Dirk, she felt embarrassed to have Leigh so close, even to comfort her. Yet she could not hold back the tears for long. Not even for Dirk. She opened her mouth wide and let out a forlorn wail that brought Leigh's arms around her tight.

She needed a shoulder and her head dropped automatically onto the nearest one. She couldn't help it if it happened to be Leigh's. She didn't give a good damn. She sobbed freely now, clutching onto Leigh, trembling in the woman's arms. Gasping, choking for breath.

She cried until she laughed—laughed at herself for the spectacle she was making, laughed at Leigh and at Dirk and at the whole rotten, mixed-up, crazy world. Most of all, she laughed at Brian, laughed at him because she could not cry any more.

Leigh handed her a paper napkin and told her to blow.

Jennie threw back her head and breathed in the cool air of on-coming night. "My apologies, everyone," she said solemnly. Then she giggled. "I think I'm a little giddy."

Leigh glanced at her husband. "Hysterical would be more like it," she said. She looked back to Jennie. "I think we'd better take you home."

"Oh, no," Jennie said quickly. She knew she sounded hysterical. Maybe she was, but the thought of climbing Mount Everest when she felt barely able to stand.... "No," she said again. "I'm having too much fun right here."

"Well..." Leigh said dubiously.

Jennie forced herself to sit up, then to get to her feet. "I'm fine," she insisted. "Just watch." She turned away from them and ran jerkily across the sand down to the water's edge. For just a moment she paused. Then she took the plunge, going down to the bottom in too shallow water and dragging her knees on the grit.

Strong fingers twined themselves through the knot of her chignon and pulled her head to the surface. She gasped for air, her body racked with sobs more convulsive than those from her tears. She felt herself lifted in strong arms and carried back up across the beach.

Dirk set her gently down on the blanket and stood beside her in the sand.

"That was quite a performance," Leigh scolded. She reached for a towel and began rubbing Jennie's back. "Without Tarzan here..." she jerked her head at Dirk, "...you'd still be on the bottom."

Jennie bowed her head selfconsciously, ashamed now to face them, to see their disapproval and disgust. She did not try to stop

Leigh, but remained silent, grateful that the woman still thought enough of her to care at all.

Dirk moved off to one side and sat down in the sand, leaning back on his hands, his long legs sprawled out. With her head still down, Jennie peered at him without turning to look at him directly. He seemed to have lost interest in her, if indeed he had had any at all beyond the need for his own fulfillment. He kept his eyes turned to the sea, his expression a study in absorbed serenity.

Dirk had hardly removed himself when she felt Leigh's touch becoming less mechanical. The towel moved around from her back, across her belly, up under her breasts. It could mean nothing, she told herself. And yet, as Leigh bent closer, touching her now with her shoulder, her breast, Jennie knew that she had not imagined the change in her manner.

She glanced up quickly at Dirk—he had not budged an inch. Leigh's hand had moved now to her thigh, massaging her gently and even through the terry cloth, communicating the urgency of her desire. Still Jennie hesitated to say anything, not wanting to arouse Dirk.

Yet when Leigh's hand moved upward from her knee, Jennie could sit still no longer. She grabbed Leigh's wrist and held it tight. "Take it easy," she murmured. "I'm not made of wood."

Leigh laughed lightly. "I was in the process of rediscovering that," she said. "Why'd you stop me?"

"Why?" Jennie said incredulously. "But . . . ." Wildly, she gestured toward Dirk.

"Oh, him," Leigh said, dismissing him completely by her tone. She shook herself free of Jennie's fingers and laid her palm against the side of Jennie's thigh.

Jennie thought that she had surely lost her senses —or maybe Leigh had. One of them was making a hideous mistake. Still, she could not deny the fact that she felt good wherever Leigh touched her. Even the wildness of her screaming nerves calmed under

Leigh's hands. If she could just let herself go, let herself relax, there would be no pain, no confusion.

"He's asleep," Leigh whispered.

Peering at him intently, Jennie realized that it must be so. He hadn't moved in many minutes. She felt a little of the hesitation beginning to wane. Yet something ticked along her nerves like the warning note of a time bomb. She held herself stiff and aloof.

Leigh's lips touched the hollow of her throat, her tongue caressed. Jennie felt the last of her resistance draining away, leaving her limp and more than willing. Her own need had gone beyond sex now, into the never-never land of tranquility. She took Leigh now as she might have taken a gallon of gin or an overdose of pills, reaching out with eager hands for the promise of oblivion.

Leigh could have done anything with her that she wanted. Killed her, if she pleased. Jennie lay in a stupor of apathy, feeling Leigh's caressing hands, her warm lips as though they brushed only against the surface of her shell and could never truly break through to the reality of her self.

Yet even in her anguish and apathy, Jennie could not deny for long the quickening sensation thrilling along her nerves, the tenseness along her thighs. Out of habit, perhaps, or maybe just out of perversity, her body began to come alive, prickling with a need she hadn't thought about or wanted to admit. As she relaxed, Leigh touched her more intimately, kissing her, kissing her. Everywhere. Everywhere. But slowly, tenderly, as though she had cherished the desire for a very long time and was loath to let go.

Suddenly Jennie felt herself going wild with need, all of her leaping eagerly to catch at the promise of fulfillment. Her body heaved and her fingers grasped convulsively at Leigh's scalp, urging her, pleading with her silently and yet eloquently for release.

When it came, she felt herself lift off the blanket, spin away into the night air to drift ... to drift like a feather, spiralling earthward, settling down among the dunes.

When she came back to earth it was more like the landing of a bomb. Looking up, she saw Dirk Whitman towering above them, standing spread-legged like an angry Colossus. She felt the blood rush to her head to blind and suffocate her. She had no idea how long he had been standing there. Nor which one of them he intended to strangle first. Terrified, she realized that she could not move to escape him if she had to.

Leigh rocked back on her heels and looked up the ridiculous distance to her husband's perspiring face. Glancing at her, Jennie realized that the woman showed no signs of fear. If anything, she looked at him more fondly now than usual.

Slowly it began to dawn on Jennie that it was she who was being taken advantage of, and not Dirk Whitman. She, lying drenched with perspiration on the sand while the gang queued up. She cursed herself that she had not understood sooner the nature of Dirk Whitman's sickness, his need to flagellate himself by watching his wife making love to someone else. Even as she recoiled in revulsion, she pitied him, knowing something of the torture he must inflict upon himself with his warped need. He would have been better off if he had stuck to Grandfather's torture devices.

Leigh's hand settled lightly onto her thigh. Still watching her husband's face, holding herself stiff and waiting.

Jennie felt the perspiration running in rivulets down her side. The blanket itched against her back. I could scream, she thought matter-of-factly, but no one would hear me. I could cry and plead for mercy. But what's the use. If he wants it now, let him have it.

Resignedly, she sighed and lay back, wanting to get it over with as soon as possible.

She heard Dirk let out a cry, like a child slapped for no good reason. Then, for a moment, there was silence. When at last she opened her eyes, Dirk was down on his knees beside her.

But it wasn't she he was after. He grabbed Leigh roughly by the shoulders and shoved her backwards onto the sand. He went to her savagely, using her mercilessly, punishing them both for God knew what sins.

Watching them, fascinated and horrified by the violence of their union, Jennie thought to herself: The man is insane. Not just a little off like the rest of us. But, by God, insane. Stark raving.

Dirk lay still finally, cradled in Leigh's arms like an infant. Jennie watched Leigh's fingers caress the bald head as a mother might pet a child, heard her crooning to him, soothing him with tenderness.

Jennie started to her feet, believing the battle was done. Behind Dirk's back, Leigh raised a hand to hold her off. And listening, Jennie heard him begin to sob.

CHAPTER THIRTEEN

Standing on the fluffy yellow bathmat, Jennie stared at herself in the full-length mirror, counting battle scars. Ugly yellow and reddish-black bruises marred the smooth flesh of her arms and legs. On her thighs, her ribs, even her buttocks, she could still make out clearly the imprint of fingertips that had dug into her. Brian's, Jake's, Dirk's, and the smaller ones that were Leigh's. How many more would she collect before she stopped running? Already she was beginning to feel like a rogue's gallery. Already the momentary excitement of each sexual encounter had taken its toll on her nerves.

She might have gone on like that, bouncing from mattress to mattress, if it hadn't been for Dirk Whitman. Seeing him last night on the beach, tearing himself to shreds, destroying himself and the woman he loved, had left her sick at heart and afraid. She realized that in her own way she was not really very different from Dirk. In a few short days, she had herself fallen from grace, wallowing in lust in an attempt to hide from herself other, more urgent problems. For the sake of her own sanity, she could not go on this way. For all the running around, the sleeping around, she had not even begun to deal with the true source of her anxiety.

Turning away quickly from the mirror, she stepped into the bedroom and began to dress. She knew what she had to do. She should have listened to Brian in the first place. Surely she could not remain in this house and expect to find any kind of sanity, although the alternatives that faced her seemed hardly more promising.

She had not yet found in herself the strength to permit her to go home to Brian. Maybe they could work something out. Even now. But she had no faith in it. Anything would be a compromise and they had both made too many already. For just a moment, when Brian had told Dirk to go to hell, she had felt a glimmer of hope for him, for them. But only for a moment. Brian had been a coward, a man without pride for too long. He would never really change.

Nor would she. For she realized now that in her own way she was probably more of a coward than he had ever been. She had always been afraid of something. Of being pregnant, of losing another child, even afraid of admitting how very much she loved and needed Brian. Now that she had lost him, she was still afraid.

She pulled open the dresser drawer and began pulling underthings out and tossing them onto the bed. She didn't have a valise, she didn't have a cent. She would have to ask Leigh for money to get back to the city, a prospect she didn't relish in the least. The less she had to do with either of them now, the happier she would be.

She went to the closet and took dresses from their hangers and draped them over her arm. It might be possible for her to hitch a ride back to the city, once she got away from the Whitman estate. She'd done it often enough and easy enough when she was younger. All she'd ever had to do was stand at the side of the road and smile and the next thing she knew, she was in the center of a traffic jam. But even the thought of that revolted her now. She was sick and tired of using her body that way. Sick and tired of sex, sick and tired of men. And of women.

As she laid the dresses out on the bed beside her underthings, she heard the door open quietly behind her. She glanced into the dresser mirror and saw Leigh, standing just inside the door and watching her. She did not turn around, but kept on with the business of getting her belongings in order.

She knew by the sound that Leigh had put on shoes for the first time since their arrival on Friday. She had already seen the tight fitting slacks and man-tailored shirt. Curiously, she wondered what the occasion might be that had sent Leigh into clothing. But she didn't intend to ask questions. Not about anything. She wanted out, as fast and painlessly as possible.

Leigh stopped a yard behind her. "You're leaving us," she said. It wasn't a question, but more a plea.

Jennie nodded.

Leigh sighed. "It's just as well," she said. She sat down on the edge of the bed and folded her hands in her lap.

"I'll have to borrow a valise," Jennie said. "Brian took ours when he left."

"Sure," Leigh said.

Jennie glanced at her, surprised at the woman's apparent apathy. Leigh had always been the one with a grin, the one who weathered every storm with a light heart. She was not smiling now, not even a little. The tone of her voice sounded like a death knell.

Laying a dress front down on the spread, Jennie began to fold it, ready for the valise. Leigh reached out suddenly and took a fold of the material between her fingers. She held it loosely, rubbing her thumb against the soft cotton.

Jennie tugged gently at the skirt of the dress and Leigh released it. Trying not to look at the woman, Jennie folded the dress and laid it aside, then she reached for a blouse.

"I don't want you to leave," Leigh said glumly. "I hope you know that."

She didn't have the strength to argue. "Don't make it any harder for me than it is, Leigh. Please," she begged.

Leigh leaned forward and took hold of her wrist. "If you stay," she said, "it won't happen again. I promise."

Jennie laughed harshly. "And I'm supposed to believe you?" she said. "I believed you last night when you told me Dirk was asleep. And you knew damned well he wasn't."

Leigh's glance did not waver. "Yes, I knew it," she said. "And I lied to you. But, I swear it, Jennifer. It won't happen again."

Jennie clucked disgustedly and turned away. "I'm not two years old, Leigh. From what I've seen, this sort of thing probably goes on a good bit of the time."

Leigh pushed herself off the bed and followed Jennie into the bathroom. She leaned against the doorjamb and watched while Jennie emptied cosmetics from the medicine cabinet.

Jennie felt Leigh watching her and her fingers trembled as she reached for a jar of cold cream. Suddenly, she spun around and faced the woman. "Don't stand there looking at me," she said irritably. "I don't want to stay and that's all there is to it."

"Not quite," Leigh said easily. "You haven't listened to my side of the story."

Jennie reached behind her and grasped the edge of the sink with both hands. She didn't want to hear Leigh's side of the story. She didn't want to listen to anything. "Please," she begged. "Let me go."

Leigh straddled the doorway and folded her arms. She looked ridiculous, standing there like a statue, defying Jennie to try to pass. Yet Jennie realized that she was no match for the woman, if Leigh honestly meant to prevent her from leaving. She sighed tiredly and relaxed against the sink.

"That's better," Leigh commented. "Now listen to me, for just a minute. You think we're running a brothel here, but you couldn't be farther from the truth. What happened this weekend happened because of you. Because of that damned painting. Dirk's had an obsession about you ever since I brought it here." She shrugged. "I guess I have too," she said. "We always have liked the same women."

"You can't tell me," Jennie said, "that this is the first time this sort of thing has gone on."

Leigh glanced away. "Dirk is a sick man, Jennifer."

Jennie leaned away from the sink. "You think I don't know it?" she said sarcastically. "After last night?"

Leigh turned her back on the sarcasm and walked into the bedroom. Watching her go, the way her shoulders slumped, the way she walked with a dragging step, Jennie remembered Brian leaning against the barricade. A twist of sympathy flashed through her, dulling for a moment the sharp pangs of her own anxiety.

She went to Leigh and rested her hand lightly on the woman's arm. "I didn't mean to be cruel," she said. "I'm just so upset myself that I forgot other people might have a few problems of their own."

Leigh smiled bleakly. "Just a few," she said. She patted Jennie's hand. "But you don't have to hear them."

Jennie took her hand and led her to the bed. They sat down together on the edge. "Talk," she ordered.

Leigh swung her legs onto the spread and stretched out on the bed. She folded her arms under her head and stared at the ceiling. "Dirk has never been completely normal," she said. "I don't think any of the Whitmans have. He's not at all dangerous. Just what you might call ... anti-social, I guess. Anyhow, he's been in trouble a few times and I was finally told either to put him away somewhere or ...."

"Or keep him out of sight," Jennie finished, understanding now why the wealthy Whitmans chose to live in the Dungeon.

"Exactly," Leigh said. "So I brought him out here. He never leaves the place. But once in a while, we have people come out just to keep him from going stir crazy." She laughed. "That's not as simple-minded as it sounds."

"I think I understand," Jennie said.

Leigh glanced at her and then away. "It's a little difficult to explain," she said. "But I'll try. He's got, along with everything else, a thing about sex. He ... he can't get it up unless he ...."

Unless he watches me making out with somebody else. Then he goes wild."

"That's awful," Jennie blurted. "He looks ...."

"I know how he looks," Leigh said bluntly. "But it doesn't mean a damn thing."

"But ..." Jennie stumbled, "...I don't understand." In her mind however she was beginning to piece it all together. The interest in Brian, the interest in herself. "What do you do?"

Leigh propped herself on one elbow, her back toward Jennie, and looked away to the window. "When he gets a thing for somebody, like he did about you, he sends me out to bring home the bacon. In your case, I couldn't even get at you except through Brian. Which is why ...." She shrugged. "And once I bring the girl home, or the man as the case may be, Dirk uses his influence to buy what he wants. It's bribery in a primitive form."

Jennie remembered suddenly Leigh's reaction to the business about the gallery. "But you tried to stop him the other day," she said. "I heard you."

Leigh was silent for a long moment. When she spoke, her voice was low and husky. "I didn't want to drag you into this mess," she said slowly. "I told you that." She fell silent once more.

Jennie thought she detected the oncoming of tears. A sound she had grown used to in herself but one that she had never expected to hear from Leigh. She leaned across to the woman and touched her shoulder. "It's all right," she said gently. "No harm's been done. I didn't come out here pure."

Leigh made a choking sound that might have been meant as a laugh.

Indignantly, Jennie withdrew her touch. "That's funny?"

"Everything's funny," Leigh said, "if you stop long enough to think about it." She rolled over and propped herself on the other arm. "The funniest thing in the world is the fact that you're the one woman in my life I ever wanted to keep all to myself. And I never had a chance."

"You married him," Jennie said sharply. "It's not my fault ...."

"I wasn't talking about the one I married," Leigh said. "I know all about what a mess I am. I was talking about you. And Brian."

Jennie stared at her incredulously. "But Brian and I are through. He's already filed for divorce."

Smiling, Leigh took Jennie's hand and raised it to her lips. "Don't you ever know what's going on, little one?" she chided. "You two can't stay away from each other any more than Dirk and I can. We're all sick that way. The whole damn human race. You get hung up on somebody and ...."

"That's what you think," Jennie said confidently. "As far as I'm concerned, I don't care if I never see Brian again as long as I live."

"You don't mean that, Jennifer."

Jennie smiled triumphantly. "Oh, don't I? She said. "I'll show you how much I mean it."

She flung herself against the woman, pushing her down to the bed. She brought her mouth down hard on Leigh's, her tongue darting between the woman's lips. Leigh's hands were against her shoulders, holding her off, but Jennie was not to be denied—not this time. This time it was she who wanted, she who would use Leigh as she herself had been used.

Her fingers fumbled with the buckle of Leigh's belt. Both Leigh's hands closed over hers. She felt the woman wriggling beneath her, trying to push her away. She rolled on top of her, pinning her down to the mattress, flattening the woman's breasts with her own. Moving her body against Leigh's, demanding that she respond.

Gradually Leigh stopped fighting. She relaxed and let her arms slide around Jennie's back to hold her tight. Returned her kisses eagerly, hungrily.

Almost before she knew what had happened, Jennie found herself being rolled onto her back. Leigh's hands went under her

skirt, tugging at her panties. She felt the touch of morning dampness on her skin as Leigh pulled her skirt up around her waist.
Then Leigh was all over her, caressing her with hands and mouth
and legs.

Something went all wrong, Jennie thought desperately. And
here I am again, right where I started, flat on my back in the
middle of a bed.

No matter how good her intentions, it always seemed to wind
up this way. Hands sliding over the perspiration on her body,
moist lips touching her in tender places, flesh meeting flesh on
rumpled sheets. She had asked for it, asked for it all. Thrown herself at Jake and at Leigh, humiliated herself with Dirk. Given herself too willingly, too eagerly to everyone but the man she loved.

She closed her eyes and bit her lower lip, holding back the
tears that even now threatened to spill over. Hating herself, hating Leigh, hating the whole world. Cursing under her breath
the body that had betrayed her, the lust she could not control.
Cursing it, yet responding to it, offering herself to the woman she
wanted to hate.

She felt the sharp, dull thrill of ecstasy as Leigh touched her.
Felt herself rise free of the earth, free of care, free even of guilt.
Felt herself give as abundantly as she had received. Felt herself
live and felt herself die a little.

Then Leigh was beside her, holding her gently and soothing
her as she had soothed her husband the night before. Crooning
softly and stroking her hair. Kissing away the tears.

"It's okay, baby," Leigh crooned. "It's all right."

She would have laughed if she could have. Laughed and told
the woman it was she who did not understand. For Jennie knew
now the source of her anguish, the cause of her tears. It was not
her own behavior that plagued her now, any more than it had
ever been, but Brian's deceit, Brian's betrayal. He had offered her
to Dirk Whitman in exchange for a showing at the Whitman
gallery. Offered her like a piece of merchandise. Still worse, once

he had done it, he didn't have the guts to go through with his end of the deal.

Thinking rapidly, Jennie began to outline in her mind a plan of revenge. She didn't care if she was being petty. Didn't give a good damn what anyone might think of her. If Brian seriously thought he would get away with dragging her name through the mud ....

She forced herself to relax in Leigh's arms, sighing and turning her head as though she were falling asleep. The easiest part of her scheme would be fooling Leigh. Leigh who loved her and wanted to protect her.

Once she had gotten rid of Leigh, it would be simple enough to find a phone and make some arrangements about getting out of this hellhole.

In a few moments, she had relaxed enough, apparently, to convince Leigh that she had indeed fallen asleep. The woman stood up very carefully so as not to disturb her and pulled on her slacks. For just a moment, she stood beside the bed. Then she leaned over and kissed Jennie gently on the side of the face. She moved away soundlessly on the thick carpeting.

The moment Jennie heard the door click shut behind Leigh, she sat up and swung herself off the bed. Straightening her skirt and smoothing back a few whisps of hair, she checked her appearance in the mirror. A little battered and a hell of a lot the worse for wear. But she'd have to make do with what she had. She tiptoed across to the door and listened for a moment for the sound of Leigh's heels along the hall.

Not satisfied that the woman was yet out of sight, she opened the door cautiously and peered up and down the hall. All was silent and apparently deserted. Still tiptoeing, just in case, she made her way down the hall to the stairs.

Once she had made the staircase, Jennie felt relatively safe. She descended quickly and made her way to the library. Scanning the room, she discovered the phone on a low table just inside the door. Taking a last hasty peek down the hallway toward the back of the house, she stepped inside and closed the door behind her.

She raised the receiver and poked a finger at the dial. Her attention was suddenly riveted to Brian's painting, hanging on the far wall directly across from her. That damned painting that had started this whole miserable business. She stared at it incredulously. It had been turned with its face to the wall and hung crookedly, as though it had been flipped over in a moment of anger. Scrawled across the back in huge black letters was her name and the number seventy-five.

It didn't take a genius to figure that she had already been removed from the active list and filed away for future reference. Yet she felt distinctly uncomfortable nevertheless. It was a little like looking at her own corpse in its coffin. Vaguely she wondered what might become of the painting, the one really good thing Brian had ever done. If she could manage somehow to buy it back from the Whitmans....

You damned fool, she thought irritably.

Resolutely, she turned back to the phone and dialled with a steady hand.

Jake answered on the first ring, as though he had been sitting by the phone waiting for her call.

As she told him her plight, Jennie became increasingly positive that he had indeed been waiting to hear from her. Waiting for her to come crawling on her knees, begging him for help. He listened to her, let her speak her piece and when she had finished, he assured her that he would be there in less than a wink.

As she hung up the phone, Jennie felt a mantle of dread fall around her shoulders. She couldn't tell what Jake might have in mind, but she knew that she was walking into a trap. And with her eyes wide open.

She turned toward the door and grasped the handle. Before she could turn it, an excited voice caught her ear. She inched the door open a crack and peered out.

In the middle of the hall, Arthur stood with his back to her, looking toward the staircase. At the foot of the stairs, looking as though the roof might have finally caved in, sat Leigh, her head on her knees, hands clutching her ankles.

"You got to do it," the old man screamed. "You got to. He's locked hisself in the cellar again."

Leigh remained motionless for a long time. When finally she moved and stood up, Jennie caught her breath. Leigh the beautiful, Leigh the serene had fallen apart at the seams. She looked haggard and very, very old, every one of her forty-five years etched deeply across the lovely face.

But she was still magnificent. Standing there like a queen, her pride, her dignity intact. She raised her chin high and peered regally down at the little old man. "All right," she said. "Call them."

CHAPTER FOURTEEN

Jennie sat alone on the terrace, gazing out past the barricade to the sea. Beside her, packed and ready to go, her earthly belongings in a valise Arthur had found for her. She felt strangely empty inside. Empty, useless, and unwanted. She was sorry now that, in the moment of her greatest need, she had not been able to offer Leigh even comfort.

She had not seen Dirk go. She had remained in her room, hovering near the door, listening as Leigh surrendered him at last to an institution. Listening as Arthur and a white-coated attendant hacked down the heavy cellar door. Listening, too, as he screamed, pleading with Leigh to save him.

For a long time she had listened to the silence. Not daring to think, to feel. Numb. Suspended in time.

Gradually, she had become aware again. Aware that she had her own life to live, her own problems to handle. Jake might show up at any minute and she knew better than to keep him waiting.

It had been over two hours now, Jennie realized, glancing at her watch. Two nightmarish hours of waiting to begin, to take up her life where she had left it only a few days before. In time she would forget the ugly, gloomy house. And Dirk. And maybe even, in time, she would forget Leigh.

But she couldn't afford to think about Leigh. Not just yet. She had no idea where the woman had gone after they took Dirk away. Perhaps down to the beach. Perhaps to her room. Jennie couldn't even say that she had made an honest effort to find her.

Instead, she had come down here to the terrace, needing to be alone with the troubled muddle of her thoughts.

She heard a car crunch onto the gravel drive and stop in front of the house. She made no move to get up, but slid down in her chair, huddling herself together. In a few moments she heard the familiar click of Jake's heels on the flagstone.

"Nobody home in this godforsaken place?" he said. "I rang the damn bell fifty times."

"I don't know where anybody is," Jennie said honestly. "There's been a little trouble."

He hunched a hip onto the stone barricade and sat with his foot swinging. "The old boy flipped his lid?"

"Yes," she said, surprised. "How did you know?"

Jake sighed. "You must lead a pretty sheltered life," he said. "Everybody's been expecting it for years."

She pushed herself out of the chair. "Would you like a drink?"

"Hell, yes," he muttered. "It's so goddamned hot, the paint's peeling off the car."

She went to the wicker bar against the wall of the house and fixed them each a double scotch on the rocks. She had learned from Brian the value of alcohol. Never in her life had she desired oblivion more.

She handed him the drink and sat down with her own on the lounge. She put her feet up and turned her face to the sun.

"What the hell's the matter with you?" Jake said. He slid away from the wall and came to stand beside her. "A couple of hours ago, you couldn't wait to get away from this place."

Jennie sighed. "That was then," she murmured.

"What?"

"Oh, nothing, Jake. I'm just tired."

The ice cubes jiggled against his glass. "Look here," he said, "I don't know what you think you're doing. But I'll tell you one thing, Jen. Don't try makin' a jackass out of me. It won't work twice."

"I know," she said. "You're too well adjusted."

He looked like he wanted to throw the drink in her face. His cheeks turned a dark, angry red and perspiration ran down the back of his neck and soaked into his collar. Raising the glass, he jerked his head back and drained the drink in one gulp.

Jennie turned away from the sight of his rage. She wasn't afraid of him anymore. She couldn't even take him seriously. She had seen too much of real trouble to be impressed by anything Jake could come up with.

He must have sensed her attitude. He sat down at the foot of the lounge, his head lowered, the empty glass between his palms. She watched him revolve the glass slowly.

"So what do you want from me?" he said after a while.

"Not much," Jennie said. "Just blood."

He glanced up at her curiously. "You know I got scotch in my veins."

She ignored his attempt at humor. "I want you to finance my divorce," she said flatly. "Brian's already filed suit on the grounds of adultery."

He whistled a shrill sound between his teeth.

She nodded. "That's right," she said. "And if you want to save your own hide, you'll help me beat him to the punch. We've got two advantages. Your money. And my helpless femininity."

Jake snorted. "You're behind the times," he said. "A woman doesn't buy what she used to."

"I didn't mean that," she said impatiently. "I can prove that Brian went to bed with Leigh Whitman. I saw it with my own eyes."

"You got witnesses?"

She started to say Dirk's name, then hesitated, realizing the futility of trying to use him as a witness. Even if they let him out of the institution, he would hardly testify against his own wife.

"That's what I thought," he said.

"Well, what's wrong with me? I saw it, after all."

Jake shrugged. "We can try," he said. "I know a lawyer who can dig up dirt about the Virgin Mary." He got up and went to fix himself another drink.

"For God's sake, stay sober," she said. "I can't drive that thing you call a car.

He emptied the glass in two swallows and banged it down on the bar. "I'm not even sure I can," he said. "But let's give it a try."

He picked up her valise and waited for her to join him. Then he turned and stalked off around the side of the house.

Jennie followed after him eagerly enough, glad to leave the place where she had seen so much unhappiness. As she rounded the corner of the house, she allowed herself a final glance over the stem facade of the mansion. Then, pulling her head high, she turned away and climbed into Jake's broken-down Ford.

She kept her eyes turned straight ahead as Jake drove away from the house and down the lane to the highway. Only for one moment, as they drove through the dark tree tunnel, did her courage waver. Then they were on the other side, trailing a cloud behind them down the dusty road.

Jennie drew a deep sigh of relief. "Thank God that's over," she said.

"What happened out there anyway," Jake said. "When I saw Brian—"

"You saw Brian?" Jennie interrupted him.

"Sure," he said. "He dropped by the place this morning and asked me for the name of an agent. Said he's going to try his hand at commercial art."

"And he didn't mention the divorce?"

Jake shrugged. "Why the hell should he? He came to ask me for a favor."

Jake's explanation sounded reasonable enough. And yet, knowing Brian, it didn't really sound right at all. He might be a coward, he might be any number of things. But that kind of bastard he wasn't.

Jennie wrapped herself in thought and Jake, his attention on traffic, mercifully let her be. The idea of Brian going in for commercial art intrigued her. It was a field he had always disparaged as a form of prostitution. But, at the same time, it was a field in which he should prove highly successful. With his superior drafting ability, his sense of color and composition, he had a definite edge over his competition. And he could make all kinds of money in the field. All kinds of alimony.

A contented smile touched the corners of her mouth. With a little luck, she could get away from Jake in no time at all. Take a place of her own and maybe have a little free time to look around. To start dating again. Maybe even find herself a man. The right man. After all, she was only twenty-four.

They drove most of the way back to Manhattan in silence. They stopped only once, for a quick bite at a roadside diner. The old car took its sweet time about the trip and it was already dark when they pulled into a parking spot near Jake's Village apartment.

Jennie opened the door for herself, knowing Jake ignored the refinements of polite behavior. At least with her. Only a few blocks away, in the house that had once been their dream, Brian probably lay on a couch in a drunken stupor, passing time in the only way he seemed to know how. Too bad about him in a way. Too bad. But that was his worry now. For herself, she had already launched herself on a new career, a new way of life. She knew what she wanted, and she intended to have it at any price. She had left no room in her scheme of things for the likes of Brian Dunbar.

Jake led the way inside and up the three flights to his apartment. The smell of garbage climbed the stairs behind them. The old building had always depressed her. She resented it, now that she would have to live in it for a while.

As Jake unlocked the door and preceded her inside, Jennie said to his back, "When are you going to move out of this dump? It gives me the creeps."

Jake swung his arm back and pitched the valise onto an over-stuffed chair. "What for?" he said. "For this rent, I couldn't get tent space in Central Park."

"But you make money," she said impatiently. "You're always collecting royalties on something or other."

"That's a laugh," Jake said. "I haven't written a decent play in three years, and the critics know it. Give me a few more months and I'll be in the same boat as Brian."

Jennie sighed. Of all the fools in the world, she must be the biggest. If you have to act like a whore, the least you could do was find a John with a bankroll. She let herself fall down onto the couch and kicked off her shoes. He had levelled with her. Now she would level with him. No more pretenses on either side.

"I'll get out of here as soon as I get some cash from Brian," she said. "In the meantime, I'll have to live off you."

He loosened the knot of his tie and opened the collar button. "Don't worry," he said. "I told you I'd keep you for as long as you wanted."

"You'll get what you pay for," she said crisply.

Jake shook his head slowly. "That's not the way I had it figured," he said. "Like I told you, kid, a woman doesn't bring what she used to. From what I know about you," he grinned, "the market value's going down all the time."

She started to get up, wanting to leap at him and scratch his eyes out of their sockets. Brian must have told him everything. Him and anybody else who wanted to listen. No wonder she had felt as if she was walking into a trap.

Jake was beside her in two strides. He grabbed her wrists and held them in a paralyzing grip. "You just take it easy," he said.

He didn't raise his voice. He didn't have to. The burning hatred in his eyes told her all she needed to know. She thought suddenly of Dirk Whitman, locked away somewhere behind bars. Dirk, who had attacked his wife so savagely in the name of love. She saw the same look on Jake's face now. A look of hatred mixed with fear, of desire tinged with revulsion.

He dragged her off the couch onto the floor and went down on her. She beat at his shoulders with her fists and tried to squirm out from under him. She heard the sound of her own voice, screaming at him, screaming.

She felt hot searing pain shoot through her. Her fingernails raked at the skin across his shoulders. The more she fought him, the more brutal he became. She whimpered, whispering Brian's name.

She didn't even hear the footsteps. But she saw the feet, planted solidly on the floor. Jake lifted off her like he had been picked up in the teeth of a derrick. She heard the sickening thud as he crashed into the wall.

She managed to struggle to her knees in time to see Brian take off in a flying leap at the pile against the wall.

Jake came violently alive, rolling away just in time to avoid being mashed by Brian's bulk. He got to his knees and for a moment supported himself on one hand.

I'd better get out of here, Jennie thought, and call the police.

She scrambled to her feet and started toward the door.

Before she had gone ten steps, Brian grabbed her arm and spun her halfway around. "You're not going anyplace," he said. "I'm not finished with you."

He shoved her backwards toward the couch. Her knees gave under her and she was back on the floor again, crouching in terror.

Brian backed off and made a slow half circle around Jake. Jake remained on his knees, watching Brian as though fascinated.

"Get the hell up from there," Brian said, "and fight like a man, you lousy son of a bitch."

Jake didn't move a muscle. The blood had drained out of his face and he looked ready to be sick any moment. Glancing from one to the other of them, Jennie wondered if Brian would attack him if he remained in his corner. She knew Brian could snap him in two, if he wanted to. Splatter him all over the wall and leave the pieces behind for the roaches. Watching him, standing there like a bull ape guarding its lair, she knew she wished that he would. Just this once. Not because it was Jake. Not because of the way Jake had abused her. But for the sake of Brian's own pride. And her pride in him.

"God damn it," Brian said hoarsely, "you act like a woman." He moved suddenly and grabbed Jake by the front of his shirt. He lifted him off the floor and set him on his feet. "I never even hit a woman when she's down."

Jennie laughed in spite of herself, a little of the tension relieved by Brian's remark. For she realized that he was, in his own way, apologizing for the scene on the Whitman's terrace.

Her relief was short-lived. Brian let go of Jake's shirt and brought his arm back. It shot forward and his fist smashed into Jake's face.

Jennie ducked her head and put her hands over her eyes. She didn't want to look. She could never bear the sight of bloodshed. Not even Jake's. But she couldn't resist the temptation, wanting to see what Brian had done to him. She spread her fingers and squinted at them.

Miraculously, Jake was still on his feet. There wasn't much left that looked like a face. Blood gushed from both lips and ran down from his nose. He opened his mouth and tried to speak. He sounded like a man at the bottom of a swimming pool.

Brian took hold of his arm and shook him. "What did you say?" he demanded.

"Go to hell," Jake croaked. His legs gave way beneath him and he sagged heavily against Brian's side.

Brian gave him a shove.

Jake's body went down like a deflated balloon. He sighed once and rolled onto his back.

Brian turned his back on Jake's unconscious form and stood towering over Jennie, his fists still clenched.

She forced herself to look up at him, terrified at what she might find in his eyes, yet even more terrified to defy him.

He was silent for a long time, his eyes searching hers. "I hope you're satisfied," he said finally.

Her eyebrows arched high, pulling wrinkles into the flesh at the corners of her eyes. "What's that supposed to mean?"

He sighed. "Leigh called me a little while ago."

"Oh, that," Jennie said imperiously. "Everyone knows Dirk's insane. He's been that way for years."

"He was insane, you mean."

She didn't like the tone in his voice. Didn't like it at all. It accused her of everything she had ever done and lots more that she hadn't. "He was all right when I left," she said helplessly.

"I don't know about that," Brian said. "And I don't give a good damn. But he's dead now. Leigh sent him to this god-damned fancy place out on the Island where they're supposed to know how to prevent accidents. But he managed to hang himself anyhow before he'd been there an hour."

"Oh, Brian," she breathed. "I'm so sorry. So sorry. And poor Leigh. She must be...."

"She is," he said crisply. He turned away from her, as though ready to leave.

Jennie leaped up from the floor and paddled after him. She grabbed hold of his arm. "Why do you blame me?" she wailed. "You took me out to that damned place."

He turned his head to look down at her. "You know, it's a funny thing about you," he said. "You always manage to blame everybody but yourself. No matter what happens."

"That's not fair," she blurted.

But it was. And she knew that he knew it as well as she did. She watched a spark of amusement come into his blue eyes.

"You want to know something funny?" he said. "I made a deal with Dirk to play romeo for his wife if he'd keep his goddamned hands off you. I even went so far as to tell him you wouldn't be interested if he tried."

"What did he say?"

Brian glanced away. "What the hell do you think he said? He laughed in my damn fool face."

She felt very close to him now, very close. If she knew him at all, he would turn to her now, for sympathy, for understanding. She would give it to him, give him all the love she felt welling up in her. Let him take her in his arms, the way he used to. And hold her.

She put her hand lightly on his arm. "Brian," she murmured, "it isn't really our fault. It would have happened anyhow, sooner or later. Leigh told me that herself."

He frowned. "So what has that got to do with anything? It happened this weekend, Jen."

"Yes, but …."

He faced her squarely now. "What the hell are you trying to do?"

She could not meet his glance. She lowered her head. "What about us?" she whispered. "Can't we …"

Brian laughed crudely. "Should we bring Jake home with us or leave him here?"

Jennie felt her cheeks go hot with rage. Still, she could not let him go. Couldn't let him walk out on her now that she needed him. She tried again. "I love you, Brian. Don't you know that?"

He shook his head. "No," he said. "I don't know it. And frankly, I don't think you even know how." He started toward the door.

She hung onto his arm, almost making him drag her with him. "I want you," she wailed. "Brian, please."

He stopped abruptly and pushed her away from him. "Tell it to him," he said, jerking his head at Jake's still form. "I wouldn't touch you with a ten-foot pole."

Before she could get out another word, he was gone.

For a moment she stared at the door, refusing to believe even now that he had really left her. Why had he bothered to come in the first place, if he hadn't meant to take her home with him? Why?

It's no use, she thought. I just don't understand him at all anymore. Maybe I never have.

Feeling hopeless, completely dejected, she walked over to Jake and peered down at his battered face. She put her toes against his ribs and shoved. His mouth fell open and he made a choking sound deep in his throat.

That was just the last straw. She threw herself face down on the couch and began to sob.

CHAPTER FIFTEEN

For three days she moped about the apartment, picking up magazines and putting them down again, dusting when she had the energy, drinking endless cups of coffee. Carrying warm soup to Jake and feeding him with a spoon. Touching a cool cloth to his forehead. Once in awhile he opened his eyes and tried to speak. But most of the time he just lay there, out cold. At first she had responded willingly to the challenge of nursing him back to health. Brian had done a pretty thorough job of putting him out of commission. Almost permanently, the doctor had said. But soon even the novelty of his condition began to pall on her. She needed diversion, something to keep her occupied so that her thoughts would not stray constantly to Brian.

But they did. No matter what she was doing. Even television couldn't hold her attention. She began to grow impatient with Jake, wanting him to hurry and get well so that she might leave. Even for a few hours.

It didn't occur to her until Thursday morning that she didn't have to sit here forever, waiting for Jake to be back on his feet. Not that she'd walk out on him while he was still unconscious. But the minute he came to and stayed that way for a little while, she could get out and start looking around for a job. She still knew a few people in the business. Harry Fulmer and Rob Krebs and ... all kinds of people who would be glad to see her back in circulation. She didn't for a minute delude herself that she could depend on Jake for anything after what Brian had done to him.

Except maybe sleeping-room on the divan. He'd be afraid to get near her now. For that, at least, she was thankful, but she understood that it meant he wanted no part of her at all.

If she got a job and a place of her own, maybe, in time, she would be able to forget Brian. Maybe. And once she got him out of her system, she might still find happiness for herself.

When she came in at noontime with a cup of broth, Jake had his eyes open. Without moving his head, he followed her progress across the room. She saw the strain around his mouth, the hard line of his lips. She knew that he had probably been lying awake for hours, thinking very much the same thoughts that she had been.

"Hi," she said cheerfully. "How do you feel?"

"Lousy," he mumbled.

She spooned out a sip of the hot broth. "This'll help."

He turned his head away from the spoon. "Hmm."

"The doctor said every three hours," Jennie said flatly. "Now, open up or I'll——"

He let her feed him half of the broth. When he had had enough, he caught the end of the spoon between his teeth and held on.

"Okay," Jennie sighed. She set the cup onto the bedside table. "Would you like something else?"

He shook his head.

"Jake, I want to talk to you about something."

He nodded.

"God, I'll be glad when you can talk," she said. "I feel like a nut."

"I can talk," Jake said quite clearly. "I just figured I was better off if I didn't."

Jennie shook her head in exasperation. "You're too much," she said. "You know damned well Brian won't come back."

"It's not Brian I'm scared of," Jake said frankly. "It's you. Everywhere you go, you leave bodies behind."

It was a grizzly way to put it. But he was right. "Well, you won't have to worry for long," she said. "I'm moving out."

"Yeah?"

"Yeah," she echoed. "I have a friend who I think'll give me a job. And I can rent a place to live for eight dollars a week. So ...."

"Uh huh," he said. "You live in one of those holes and you'll be shackin' up with some other guy in a week. You might just as well stay here."

"You don't want that either," she said honestly. "And besides, I lived most of my life in one of those flea bag rooms. You'd be surprised how tough I am."

Jake made a face that was probably a grin. "Huh uh," he said. "But I've got my doubts."

It wasn't many days before Jennie was about ready to agree with him. Finding a job proved a cinch. Harry Fulmer had taken her into the shop instantly and started teaching her the latest techniques in theatrical make-up. She had found a place to live almost as easily, paying for the week's rent with the advance Harry had given her. The superficial things, the money-making and the money-spending, had come along as easily as she could have hoped, it was the other areas of her life that remained empty and touched her every moment with a sense of futility.

Standing in the shop hour after hour, curling hair and bleaching hair and peroxiding milady's moustache, she could not keep her thoughts on the monotonous routine. Time and again, she found herself considering her years with Brian, remembering sometimes only the good, sometimes the bad. But always remembering, and always regretting. Even alone in her apartment at night, she could not let it go for a minute. All the thoughts she hadn't wanted to think when she should have came rushing in on her now, like a never-ending torrent of lava. She found it increasingly difficult to sleep, to eat. To do anything beyond the purely mechanical functions of her job.

Finally a glimmer of wisdom began to shine through the fog in her brain. A ray of hope. Or perhaps merely of self-preservation. She began to understand a little of herself, some of the much that she had not dared face about herself ever before. Her selfishness, her complete lack of consideration. Not only for Brian, but for all who had loved her. For Leigh. And, yes, even for Jake. She had never once given her trust, never once given her support and encouragement. Only her body. Only her own lust for satisfaction, her greed.

She turned from the ugly woman who had come to her for a beautiful face and peered at herself appraisingly in the oval mirror. She wasn't proud of the thoughts that had been going through her head. Not proud at all. But they were her. All the her there had ever been. And maybe, even now, if she went to Brian . . . .

The moment she was free for the day, Jennie hurried outside and hailed a cab. She gave the driver the address of the house that had once been home and settled back for the long ride downtown.

She could tell him she had just come back to pick up her things, if he asked why she had come. He could hardly deny her the right of her own clothing, the few belongings she cherished. And if he let her into the house at all, it shouldn't be too difficult to make him listen to her. She couldn't be sure that he wanted to hear anything she might have to say. She didn't really care. But she had to say it. Say it all. All the shame and the guilt and the disappointment she felt in herself and in him. If he loved her at all, if he had ever loved her, he would listen.

The cab turned onto the familiar street and she felt a twist of pain go through her. It had been hardly three weeks. No time at all, when you thought about it. And yet it felt like eternity. The ugly pink facade of the house, the potted plants in the front window that he had forgotten to water. The broken pane in the front door. All the little things that had never seemed very important overwhelmed her now.

She stood on the sidewalk, looking up at the front of the house. The skylight in his studio was propped open with a stick. It surprised her a little to see it. As though she had expected his life to be as empty without her as hers had been without him. As though she had expected him to sit in a corner and wait, as she had been doing. Not really, but it seemed that way. The job she didn't really want, the shabby little room that depressed her out of her wits. They seemed somehow unreal.

She found the key in her purse where it had been since the afternoon she left with Brian and inserted it into the lock. Even the sound of a key turning in a lock, she thought. Even this can be important. When it's home.

She pushed open the door and crossed the threshold cautiously, almost as though she expected him to jump out at her from behind a piece of furniture. The downstairs smelled musty and unaired and, glancing about the living room, she realized that he hadn't cleaned the place since she left. She had a sinking feeling, as though her heart had dropped into her shoes. What if he hadn't changed? What if she found him upstairs, sprawled senseless on the bed in an alcoholic stupor? Would she love him then? Was it Brian she loved really or only the Brian she dreamed about, the one who could tell Dirk Whitman to go to hell and smash Jake's nose all over his face?

Taking a deep breath, determined to find him no matter where he was, and to love him, no matter what condition he might be in, Jennie climbed the stairs to the second floor.

As she approached the landing, she heard him moving about on the floor above, in his studio. Inching open the door, she cocked her head to the opening and listened.

His voice came down to her loud and clear. "Not that way. Turn over onto your back."

Feeling suddenly ill, Jennie grabbed hold of the edge of the door and held on tight. Waves of nausea gripped her stomach. So this was what she had come crawling home to, was it? For this she had worried herself half out of her mind? The futility of it all rushed in on her. She took a deep breath and turned to leave.

"Will this do?" a feminine voice asked.

She knew that one, too, knew it intimately. Had heard it whispering words of love to her through the long hours of a summer night. Surprised at hearing it here, she paused and listened again.

She waited a long time, huddled in her corner at the foot of the attic stairs. Yet she didn't hear another word. She didn't hear anything. Whatever they were doing up there, they'd had time enough. Cautiously she crept up the stairs, testing each step before setting her weight upon it, wanting to take them by surprise. She hadn't the vaguest notion what she would do when she got face to face with them. But she'd think of something. And she'd make damn sure it would be something Brian would remember for the rest of his life.

Steadying herself against the wall, Jennie poked her head above the level of the floor and peered into the room.

At the far end, directly under the glare from the open sky light, Leigh lay on her back, one knee up, the other leg straight. And fully dressed. Ten feet away from her Brian stood at his easel, a brush in his hand.

Jennie gasped involuntarily and instantly clapped her hand over her mouth.

But too late. Leigh sat bolt upright on the raised platform and peered in her direction.

Feeling foolish, ashamed to have let them realize that she had been deliberately spying on them, Jennie climbed the three steps to the top and came into full view.

"Well, hi," Leigh said.

Brian didn't even turn around. "If that's who I think it is," he said to Leigh, "ask her what she wants."

Leigh looked back at Jennie. "He says to ask you what you want," she repeated.

"I heard him," Jennie snapped at Brian's back. "And you can tell him that I don't want anything from him at all. I came back for my clothes."

"Tell her they're not up here," Brian said.

Leigh laughed and stood up. "If you two don't mind," she said, "I don't particularly enjoy playing referee." She glanced at Brian. "I'll be out at the house for the rest of the week. I'm closing the place up for good."

"Well, that's the best news I've heard in a long time," Brian said. "Where'll you be staying?"

"I don't know yet," Leigh said. "But I'll keep in touch."

Jennie stepped out of the way to let her pass.

Leigh paused and looked at her silently for a long time. Then she smiled and for a moment there was some of the old Leigh in her eyes. "I'm glad you came home," she said at last. "We've missed you, Jennifer." She reached out then and squeezed Jennie's hand.

And then she was gone, down the stairs and on down to the first floor.

Alone with Brian at last, Jennie felt far less sure of herself than she had even imagined. She started a dozen times to say something, one of the speeches she had been rehearsing for him all afternoon. But each time, the words seemed foolish and inadequate, not half encompassing all she meant to say.

"Well?" he said finally. "I thought you came for your clothes."

"Brian—" she started and broke off abruptly.

He refused to look at her. Stepping back from the easel, he surveyed the work he had done and nodded his approval. "Come take a look at this," he said.

Obediently she went to stand by his side. The painting on the easel was far different from anything she had seen him do before. Two girls in next to nothing sprawled together on a bed, their intentions toward each other more than obvious. She stared at it for a long time, trying to make sense out of his peculiar choice of subject.

"It's for a paperback book," he said. "I got a commission to do five in the next two months."

"But, I don't understand," she said. "You always told me ...."

"It ought to work out pretty well," he said, as though he hadn't heard her. "I'll make enough dough on these five to hold us for about six months. And that should give me plenty of time to get some serious painting done before I have to come back to this."

She hardly listened to the words. She had heard only one clearly. The *us* that had slipped out so casually, as though he had never stopped thinking in terms of the two of them. A rush of warmth, of tenderness suffused her. Still she hesitated to touch him, afraid even now of rejection.

"And by that time," Brian went on, "Dirk's estate ought to be settled and we'll be able to get away from the city."

"What's Dirk's estate got to do with us?" Jennie said curiously.

For the first time, he looked at her. "What makes you think I was talking about you?"

"But you said *us*. I heard you."

Brian sighed. "I was talking about Leigh. She's planning to open a sort of retreat for artists someplace in the mountains. I've agreed to go in with her and be an instructor or manager or whatever she needs." He shrugged. "It's the best she can find to do with herself now that she hasn't got Dirk to look after."

"She really loved him, didn't she?" Jennie breathed, remembering the woman's collapse on the day of Dirk's suicide.

"Yes," he said quietly. "I've never known anyone quite like her. And I didn't really know her at all until after ...." He turned his hand palm up. "When I think of what she's been through in the past twenty years, I feel like a goddamned fool every time I start to complain about something."

"I guess we've both learned a lot from Leigh," Jennie said quietly. "I know I have."

He looked at her for a long moment. "Yeah," he said finally.

He moved toward her then and she thought he meant to take her in his arms. She tilted her face expectantly for his kiss.

Instead, he took her by the hand and led her to the raised platform under the skylight. "Lie back and prop yourself on one hand," he said. "And smile."

She felt as if she didn't have a smile left in her, but she managed something passable and leaned back stiffly in the pose he wanted.

"That's good," he said, taking his place behind the easel. "Now, don't move." He picked up a brush and dabbed it into a smear of paint on the stained palette. "Now close your eyes and look sexy."

Her arm had fallen asleep and prickles of irritation itched along the side of her neck. Still he did not call a halt. She could hear the sound of his breathing, the sound of him moving occasionally to lift a fresh dab of paint onto the canvas. The afternoon sun baked through the skylight.

When she was about ready to faint, she heard him lay down a brush.

"Okay," he said. "That ought to do it."

She sat up stiffly and rubbed the muscle of her right arm. Damn him and Leigh Whitman together. She could get along very well without either of them. If he thought she had come here....

"You know," he said, "I could use you for a model." He reached behind him to a pile of paintings.

She saw the name and number on the back of the canvas and here in the studio, recognized them easily enough as Brian's own markings.

He turned the painting around and propped it against the wall. "Leigh gave it back to me," he said.

"I'm so glad," Jennie murmured.

"Yeah," Brian said. "It's the best thing I've ever done."

Suddenly she had had enough. One more lousy crack out of him and she'd smash the damned painting over his head. "Sometimes I hate you," she blurted. "Can't you ever think of anything but——

"Sometimes," he interrupted. "But I'm a busy man, Jen. I've got this silly wife who keeps threatening to divorce me and ... ."

Jennie gasped. "But, Brian, you said ... ."

"Yeah, I heard me say it," he said levelly. "That was then."

"And now?" she breathed.

He grinned. "Why don't you come over here and find out?"

She flung herself into his arms. As he held her close, she felt the tears start to well up in her eyes. She knew it was right for them now. Right as it had always been for them, even when it was all wrong.